The Woman Smacked The Softball With Everything She Had.

With a rebel yell, she took off, her red dress plastered to her body as she ran.

Abel grabbed the stone in his pocket and felt something strange flash up from inside his own body. He didn't realize he'd moved, but suddenly he was standing squarely in her path. She slammed into him with the force of a runaway train. He grunted and flung his arms wide to catch his balance, but it was no use. Together, they hit the ground and rolled in a tangle of arms and legs. Suddenly Abel had his arms full of her—a hot, explosive, laughing woman.

Her hair had come loose and cascaded around her head with an intoxicating fragrance. Abel could feel her heartbeat thumping in her breast as he stared down into a pair of fiery green eyes, a startled mouth, a beautiful face. It was a face that would be carved in his mind for eternity.

"I want to make love to you," he said.

Dear Reader:

Welcome to the world of Silhouette Desire. Join me as we travel to a land of incredible passion and tantalizing romance—a place where dreams can, and do, come true.

When I read a Silhouette Desire, I sometimes feel as if I'm going on a little vacation. I can relax, put my feet up and become transported to a new world . . . a world that has, naturally, a perfect hero just waiting to whisk me away! These are stories to remember, containing moments to treasure.

Silhouette Desire novels are romantic love stories— sensuous yet emotional. As a reader, you not only see the hero and heroine fall in love, you also feel what they're feeling.

In upcoming books look for some of your favorite Silhouette Desire authors: Joan Hohl, BJ James, Linda Lael Miller and Diana Palmer.

So enjoy!

Lucia Macro
Senior Editor

NANCY MARTIN

READY, WILLING AND ABEL

SILHOUETTE *Desire*

Published by Silhouette Books New York

America's Publisher of Contemporary Romance

SILHOUETTE BOOKS
300 East 42nd St., New York, N.Y. 10017

ISBN: 0-373-05590-0

First Silhouette Books printing September 1990

Printed in the U.S.A.

Books by Nancy Martin

Silhouette Intimate Moments

Black Diamonds #60

Silhouette Desire

Hit Man #461
A Living Legend #522
Showdown #576
Ready, Willing and Abel #590

NANCY MARTIN

has lived in a succession of small towns in Pennsylvania, though she loves to travel to find locations for romance in larger cities in this country and abroad. Now she lives with her husband and two daughters in a house they've restored and are constantly tinkering with.

If Nancy's not sitting at her word processor with a stack of records on the stereo, you might find her cavorting with her children, skiing with her husband, or relaxing by the pool. She loves writing romance and has also written as Elissa Curry.

One

King Kimimungo, exalted ruler of a South Pacific paradise no bigger than the island of Manhattan, raised his pudgy, bracelet-laden arms aloft to show his treasure to the gathered crowd of loinclothed natives. "I present this gift to our respected friend, Professor Abel Fletcher!"

At least, that's what he was supposed to say. In reality, the slightly inebriated island despot burped once and growled, "I presen' 'iss giff to re—re—respecked frenn, 'Fessor Abel Flessher."

The mob whooped and pounded their spears on the dried mud of the jungle floor while Abel made a stab at graciously accepting his dubious honor on behalf of the civilized world. Most of his audience wore bones in their noses, and the king himself was bedecked in a necklace of shrunken heads. But at least they recognized a real man when they saw one, because they were gazing rapturously at Abel as if he were Abe Lincoln and Muhammad Ali rolled into one. Of course he looked damned dashing, if Abel did say so himself— his leather flight jacket unzipped to reveal his manly chest, the bush trousers fashionably loose and still stained from his adventure in the jungle, the hand-some-looking stubble on his face, which wasn't a bad face, mind you, though he wasn't going to put Robert Redford out of a job. And, of course, he was a foot taller than any other human being in sight, which went a long way toward his being viewed as larger than life to these not-very-savage savages.

Another native, a pygmy-sized gentleman Abel had come to call Mickey Rooney but who was actually the king's loyal bodyguard and general secretary, trans-lated the rest of the ceremony for Abel.

In a stentorian voice, he said, "This stone has been passed down through generations to royal kings of the island of Kimi Lau from the great God of Love who hides in the volcano."

"Who?" asked Abel, struggling to understand the translation over the chatter of the crowd and King Kimimungo's singsong babble.

Mickey shushed him. "The God of Love put his great magic into this stone, Professor Abel Fletcher. The man who holds this stone in his possession will capture the woman of his eternity."

"What?"

"His woman of destiny, his—oh, hell," said Mic-key, "his babe for life, man. You know what I mean? King says you keep this stone and the first lady you touch will become your sex slave forever."

Abel burst out laughing. "Are you kidding me?"

"Very serious magic, this stone," Mickey assured him. "Don't you wonder, man, how come a jerk like the king has got himself seventeen of the most gorgeous babes on this island for his wives?"

Chuckling, Abel said, "Okay, okay. Hand it over, big guy."

The king blathered for another minute, playing to the crowd and holding onto a little painted stone like it was a piece of the True Cross. At last he gave Abel a stern look and pointed commandingly to the ground at his bare feet.

"Oh, for crying out loud," Abel muttered, but he obeyed the king's unspoken command and kneeled before the monarch. "Let's get this over with, chum, how about it? I've got a plane to catch."

The king glared into Abel's face and spoke once more.

His translator said, "Professor Abel Fletcher, His Majesty is grateful for everything you've done to help his people while you're here, so he's giving you this magic charm. Its magic has provided His Royalness with forty-nine children, so he figures it ought to help you get one or two."

"Is that an insult, pal?"

"The stone will work its magic on the first woman you touch, Professor Abel Fletcher, so he says don't go touching any of his wives before you leave."

"No problem, believe me."

"And if you should want to break the spell," Mickey continued, "you must return to this place and take it to the cave of the Love God to explain yourself."

"Right, right," said Abel. "Can I go now?"

The King suddenly grabbed Abel's right hand, and with surprising strength, he turned it palm up. Still glaring, he slapped a smooth, oblong stone into Abel's hand. In English he said, "You be careful with this magic. Powerful magic. Very powerful."

Abel looked at the little stone in his hand. It was about three inches long and as smooth as if it had tumbled in a mountain stream for centuries. Some island artisan had painted a series of tiny figures on both sides of the stone, but Abel didn't take time to study them at that moment. He pocketed the stone and stood up. "Well, it's real nice, fellas. Thanks. Now, I've got to run."

"Very good, Professor. A canoe awaits you." Mickey pointed at a tiny carved boat that bobbed on the surface of the oily black river that would wind its way to the ocean, just half a mile away.

"Uh, thanks," said Abel. "But I think I'll take the land route."

"Through the jungle, Professor? But the snakes! The poisonous bugs! The river is much safer."

But the river was water and it would lead to even more water, and if there was one thing on the earth that gave Abel Fletcher a deathly case of the queasies, it was little boats on big, deep water. Little boats had a way of tipping over and dropping their contents to Davy Jones's locker. He would never admit such weakness, of course. He thumped Mickey on the shoulder and said in his booming voice, "The safer route isn't always the best route, my good fellow. Sometimes a man's got to do what a man's got to do."

The natives didn't know what a stupid cliché that was. They just applauded and cheered and generally looked impressed while Abel strode into the snake-infested jungle and set off for civilization.

It wasn't until he was on the plane headed back to the States that he remembered King Kimimungo's silly stone. He got it out of his pocket and was sitting in first class looking at it, when a lovely young flight attendant leaned over his seat.

"Isn't that a cute souvenir! What is it?"

She had a pretty smile and a body that could make grown men weep, so Abel gave her a roguish grin and said, "It's a love charm. Want to see if it works?"

She dimpled and giggled and said, "I don't have a layover in Washington this time, but maybe I could call you next time I'm in town."

"Sure!" Abel scribbled his phone number on a cocktail napkin and passed it to the pretty young woman. But as she took the napkin in her long, manicured fingers, Abel remembered the warning of the Kimi Lauan king and quickly jerked his own hand back to avoid physical contact with the flight attendant.

She looked surprised at his abrupt recoil. "Something wrong?"

"Uh, no," Abel said, feeling like a fool but at the same time relieved that he hadn't touched her. She was nice to look at, but suddenly Abel was sure she wasn't the kind of woman he wanted around for the rest of his life. And he couldn't help thinking better safe than sorry just in case the magic did work.

She frowned at him. "If I don't turn you on, you could have just said so."

"It wasn't that! I—Hey—" But she was gone, stalking down the plane's aisle. For the rest of the flight, she ignored Abel.

Surprisingly enough, he was relieved. Abel didn't have time for women.

* * *

"So that's the whole story," he said to his colleague back in Washington. "That's where this little trinket came from."

Oliver was hunched forward in one of the leather chairs in Abel's dark, cavern of an office in the warrenlike basement of the Smithsonian Museum. Wearing a Hard Rock Café T-shirt and long hair pulled into a ponytail, Oliver was hardly the average museum employee. Perhaps that's why he and Abel got along so well.

Oliver sat back from looking at the stone on Abel's desk. "Well, it's a nice memento of your trip, I suppose. We were worried you weren't going to make it back this time—especially after we lost radio contact. The boss was furious."

"A little rage will do him good. It clears out the arteries."

"You could have sent a postcard."

"You can't buy stamps in the jungle." Abel waved his hand dismissively, sending cigar smoke wafting in the air. "When have I ever failed on a mission?"

"Never, but—well, there's always a first time. How old are you now, anyway? Forty?"

"My age has nothing to do with it," Abel snapped, unwilling to reveal to his young colleague that he'd passed his forty-first birthday not long ago and that even his bones ached from the punishing work. Bringing exhibits to the museum was getting tougher all the time but he'd never admit it. He poured brandy from the bottle he kept in his desk drawer. "I had no trouble bringing this plane back. It's sitting in the restoration room right now—in perfect shape."

Oliver grinned impishly. "I can't wait to see it."

"Have a drink first." Abel pushed the glass across his cluttered desk. He hadn't even changed his clothes yet. His leather jacket and heavy twill bush trousers still smelled of volcanic ash and ocean breezes. He needed a haircut, a decent meal, and a look at a real newspaper, but all that could wait a little longer. For a while he wanted to revel in triumph—and the envy of his desk-bound colleague.

The expedition to the far Pacific island of Kimi Lau to locate and recover a World War II bomber from the mountaintop where it had crashed decades ago had been Abel's baby from the beginning, and he'd loved every minute. For months he'd camped in the steamy jungle with his native bearers, hauling tons of gear up the mountain with a crude block and tackle, digging into the mud with his bare hands sometimes, crating the precious bits of broken airplane for the journey home. Now the plane was sitting safely in the Air and Space Museum's restoration facility just a short drive from Abel's Smithsonian office.

But instead of dashing off to another great adventure, Abel was chained to a typewriter to write a report for his superior, a thought that dampened his high spirits for a moment. He took a long swallow of fine, aged brandy, the first liquor he'd had in months, and glanced appreciatively around the room.

Abel's office was a perfect hideaway from the many stuffed shirts who worked upstairs. It wasn't terribly neat, though it did reflect a certain scholarly bent that was part of Abel's character. Books, papers, and journals of all description were scattered everywhere. A length of bone from a long-dead bull elephant did service as a paperweight, and assorted tarnished artifacts Abel had picked up on his travels were strewn around the room. The golden glow of a shaded brass lamp illuminated the walls where several aged photos of famous explorers were haphazardly pinned alongside posters of rock and roll legends. Admiral Peary seemed to be taking aim at Smokey Robinson through his telescope.

"You ought to clean up this place," Oliver said, noting the direction of Abel's glance. "It might improve your image."

"My image?"

"You could be the Errol Flynn of the museum set, the Indiana Jones of Washington. You ought to have a fancy hi-tech office with a view of the monuments to attract some women."

Abel grinned around the stub of his cigar, knowing he was due for a lecture concerning Oliver's favorite pursuit. Though a serious archeologist by training, Oliver's young brain was frequently occupied by more earthly endeavors than the lofty, academic concerns of most museum curators.

Oliver said, "You could have women swooning at your feet, if you'd let them. But you're too busy with your adventuring to notice. It's *spring*, for crying out loud!"

Abel grinned. "Hay fever season, right?"

Oliver looked outraged for a moment, then realized he was being teased. He grinned. "The itch that I'm feeling these days certainly isn't in my nose."

Abel laughed. "Tell me, Oliver, do you ever spend an hour without thinking about the fairer sex?"

"We're talking about *you* at the moment. What do you do with your spare time? Play racquetball with that doddering neighbor of yours? Tinker with that old airplane you keep in your garage? Don't you ever have a date?''

"Of course I do."

"Since Elizabeth, I mean. Are you still upset about that old romance?''

"That was over years ago," Abel said shortly. And it was true. Elizabeth had been a focal point in his life for a long time, but she'd gone to Europe for a sabbatical and never returned. He hadn't fallen apart when she left. That wasn't his style. He'd thrown himself into his work with renewed vigor, and it had paid off. His life was exciting—a constant string of new challenges.

"My love life is none of your business," he said. "I can assure you I haven't become a monk.''

Oliver studied him for a moment, "Okay," he said. "I'll back off—if you can tell me when you last had a date.''

"I've been in the jungle, dammit!''

"And before that?''

"I spent six months in France, as you well know.''

"Romancing a few *jeunes filles* along the Champs-Elysées?''

"I was digging a Spitfire out of a pasture. I was on a job!''

"And listening to the lowing of cows at night instead of seducing the farmer's daughter! My Lord—women were practically kissing your boots when you got back from that Egyptian excursion. When was your last date? Tell me and I'll leave you alone.''

Abel scowled. But he indulged Oliver by trying to remember. Trouble was, he *couldn't* recall the last time he'd seen a woman socially. There had been a few women since Elizabeth—quick, satisfying sex combined with a few entertaining evenings of intelligent conversation or cultural exchange—but he just couldn't seem to recall any one woman in particular. His scowl deepened. "I know I saw someone not long ago. I'll remember her name in a minute. Let's see—"

"Admit it," said Oliver. "You're out of practice."

"I am not!"

"It sneaks up on guys your age, you know. One day you're happily playing the field, and the next thing you know, you've forgotten how. I tell you, Abel, a saw gets rusty if you don't use it regularly."

Abel cursed colorfully.

"Maybe that stone will help," his friend said.

They both looked at the little rock on the desk.

It looked like an ordinary pebble, except for the figures painted on it. Abel picked up the smooth stone again and automatically held it up to the lamplight frowning at the meaningless hieroglyphics on its surface. The series of oddly shaped figures on both sides of the stone had been done with a strange kind of paint that reflected the colors of the room around them and showed no signs of wearing off. There was no guessing how long ago the shapes had been painted. They were crudely drawn and had no distinct shape. At least at first.

Turning the pretty piece over in his hand, Abel began to see the figures differently. They seemed to move, to change. He blinked, then frowned.

"What do you make of this, Oliver?"

"Well," his colleague began to enthusiastically spout information without even glancing at the stone, "love charms are pretty common in that part of the world. Did you know that people of Kimi Lau have thirteen festivals every year to celebrate fertility?"

"I don't need any help in that department, thank you."

"No doubt fertility is just an added bonus," Oliver said, looking amused. "But most love charms are meant to help the owner find his or her mate for life—in your case, a woman you can satisfy completely and vice versa. I'm not a fan of monogamy, but it's a pleasant notion."

Abel couldn't stop himself from studying the stone. He turned it over in his hand, savoring how the smooth bit of rock fit perfectly into the groove of his palm. It felt warm against his skin—as though the sun had imbued it with a kind radiance. Once again, the painted figures seemed to dance before his eyes.

Oliver said, "You almost believe it, don't you?"

Abel sat up quickly. "Don't be silly."

His friend peered into Abel's face. "It's true, I think. There's a part of you that's just a little afraid the magic stone might work."

"I'm not afraid of anything!"

Oliver laughed. "Maybe not snakes or rioting natives or jungle heat or any of the things that make the rest of us tremble in our boots, but you're worried about that little piece of rock! You're afraid you just might find a woman who will interest you more than your precious work."

"See here," Abel began.

"Oh, relax!" Oliver said, laughing as he got to his feet. "Spring is in the air! What could be more romantic than cherry blossom time along the Potomac? Why don't you gather up your courage and see if there's one woman on the face of the earth who could make you as happy as a bunch of old airplanes do? Let the stone work its magic on you."

"Magic," Abel muttered derisively.

But as Oliver left, Abel was oddly unable to tear his eyes off the thing. It was mesmerizing. The longer he looked, the more erotic the tiny drawings became. He found himself feeling decidedly homesick for Kimi Lau—and oddly aroused at the same time. He tilted the rock toward the light and sat in silence, smoking and studying the thing. Or maybe it was his own heart he was looking into.

Abruptly he thrust the stone into his pocket. "This is stupid," He muttered to himself.

Time to go home and get some rest.

Abel stood up, snapped off the desk lamp, locked his office, and strode quickly through the labyrinthine corridors of the museum, his loud, rapid footsteps echoing in the empty hallways. Outside, the evening breeze hit him in the face. A spring storm was in the wind, and the crisp, electrically charged air smelled fresh and exciting. Thunder rumbled overhead, so Abel hurried across the tree-lined Mall in the shadow of the Washington Monument, heading for his parked car. The pungent perfume of blossoming cherry trees filled his head. A few tourists were snapping pictures of the reflecting pool and the distant Capitol dome, and Abel brushed past them quickly.

Only when he approached the grassy Ellipse behind the White House did Abel slow his space. On the Ellipse, some people were playing softball, trying to finish their game before the storm descended. Men and women of assorted ages and sizes, all dressed in college sweatshirts and a variety of mismatched sport clothes, were yelling and laughing as they played. Abel knew all the congressional offices had teams, and a ragtag league had been set up so the office-bound workers could play off a little of the steam that tended to build up on Capitol Hill. Games were a typical sight around Washington in the spring. But something made Abel slow down this time.

He drew closer and heard the voices of the people on the grass.

"C'mon, Miss Wyatt!" yelled one man. "Let's see you hit a ball for us!"

"Yeah, try one, Miss Wyatt! You can do it!"

It was impossible not to notice the woman they were yelling at. Standing on the sidelines, she was tall and slender and dressed for anything but softball. Her dress was prim and professional and elegant—bright red with a simple gold necklace at her throat, high-heeled black pumps, and an expensive looking raincoat cast around her shoulders. Her briefcase was polished cowhide. A cloud of black hair—black as a clear, midnight sky over the desert—was pulled stiffly back from her aristocratic face. She looked close to forty years old—a grown woman who was beautiful and in control.

Abel stood on the sidewalk, transfixed by the sight of her—a woman totally unlike any he'd ever known.

"What d'you say, Miss Wyatt? Ever play softball before?"

"Try hitting one, Miss Wyatt!"

Judging by their voices, her tormentors obviously believed the woman couldn't hit a softball with a pickup truck.

She smiled and called, "All right, just this once."

She peeled off her raincoat and laid it carefully on a nearby bench. Then she kicked off her shoes and picked up a bat that had been lying on the ground. She took a couple of graceful, ladylike practice swings, but Abel saw there was a hint of strength in the way she handled herself, too. Beneath the red dress, her hips moved with a subtle twist as she swung the bat.

Abel swallowed hard and watched, enthralled.

Her teammates cheered lustily as she stepped up to the plate. The opposing team jeered in the outfield. Abel saw that there were two men on base, and from the excitement demonstrated by both teams, he guessed the contest was in its final inning. The elegant, dark-haired beauty had the power to win or lose the game.

With some surprise, Abel realized that the man standing on the pitcher's mound was none other than the vice president of the United States. The woman in red wasn't the least bit intimidated.

The vice president tossed the ball up and down in his mitt and yelled, "Think you can get a hit off me, Wyatt? Or are you one of those girls who bunts when the going gets tough?"

"Let me put it this way, sir," she called back in a low, whiskey voice so rich that Abel quivered at the sound. She asked, "How fast can you duck?"

The outfield shouted a few insults, but the woman didn't care. She settled into her batting stance and waited.

Clowning, the vice president wound up like a show-man—and made the fatal mistake of hanging a fat meatball over home plate.

The woman smacked the ball with everything she had. The vice president yelped and ducked indeed, but the force of her hit sent the ball sailing high over the heads of the horrified infield. The woman's team-mates leaped off the bench and began screaming their lungs out.

"Way to hit it, Miss Wyatt! Now *run*, damn you!"

"Go, go, go! *Go*, Samantha!"

With a rebel yell, Samantha went, her red dress plastered to her body as she ran. Sprinting to first base, she tagged the bag and then pounded down the line for second with her tumbled hair streaming out behind. The centerfielder missed the catch, so she tore past second base, rounded third and headed for home. Her teammates shrieked. The opposing team howled.

Abel grabbed the stone in his pocket and felt something queerly swordlike flash up from inside his own body. Samantha flew across home plate, going too fast to stop herself.

Abel didn't realize he'd moved, but suddenly he was standing squarely in her path. She slammed into him with the force of a runaway train. He grunted and flung his arms wide to catch his balance, but it was no use. Together, they hit the ground and rolled in a tangle of arms and legs. Suddenly Abel had his arms full of her—a hot, explosive, laughing woman.

As she tumbled, she instinctively wrapped her arms around his shoulders, hooking one leg around his hips until they came to a hard, thumping landing on the grass. Then Abel found himself squarely on top of her, pinning a very startled, beautiful woman to the ground.

They stared at each other—both out of breath, full of adrenaline and instinctively clutching each other for dear life. Their noses were two inches apart, their eyes wide. Her hair had come loose and cascaded around her head with an intoxicating fragrance. Abel could feel her heartbeat thumping beneath her breast as he stared down into a pair of fiery green eyes, a startled mouth, a beautiful face. It was a face that would be carved in his mind for eternity.

He said, "I want to make love to you."

Two

___

Samantha Wyatt's head reeled—her normally very steady, unshakable head—but she could feel the solid hunk of man against her body. Her arms were clasped around his shoulders as he pressed into her curves with the rough intimacy of a longtime lover. His hard knee jammed her thighs apart, his rough leather jacket scraped her skin. His face, unshaven and rugged, finally swam into focus.

He stared down at her with the hungry intensity of a wild animal and Samantha felt a jolt as powerful as an electrical current. Underneath the stubble, his face was further toughened by a scar that angled across his chin. A lick of dark brown hair tilted from a sharp widow's peak and brushed the slant of his heavy brows. It was a taut face—strong and determined. And his expression was deadly serious.

Samantha hoped she'd misunderstood the words he'd practically growled at her. "I—I beg your pardon?"

With the same charge of intensity, he said, "I want to carry you off and make love for the rest of the night."

She gulped and tried to laugh. "I don't even know you!"

"That doesn't matter," he said in a husky voice. "We were meant for each other. It's fate. Destiny."

Samantha braced her hands against his shoulders. "This is some kind of joke, right? I knew I shouldn't have hit that ball! Who put you up to this?"

"We belong together, Samantha."

"We do?"

"I can feel it."

"*I'd* like to feel solid ground under my feet, if you don't mind."

His hands tightened on her. "I want you. Right here. Right now."

"In plain sight of the *White House*?"

He bent closer, his mouth hovering over hers, his silver-gray eyes afire. In a moment he was going to kiss her! Samantha jammed her hands between their chests. "Hold it, buster! I don't know who you think you are, but you'd better let me up this minute. Unless you plan to magically disappear before my team gets here."

"Magic?"

He stared at her with absolute astonishment—as if she'd said something that had finally penetrated his Neanderthal brain.

In the next second, they were engulfed by the rest of her teammates. Laughing and asking her if she was all right, they milled around and pulled the handsome stranger off Samantha. Then an office mate hauled her to her feet, and Samantha dazedly accepted the congratulations of her teammates.

"Way to go, Miss Wyatt!"

"Heck of a hit, Samantha!"

She yelped as someone tried to brush the grass and bits of mud off her backside. At that moment, the vice president made his way through the throng to shake her hand.

"I never expected you to be big league material, Wyatt."

"You should know better than to underestimate me by now, sir," she replied, surreptitiously trying to brush the stains from the back of her dress.

He laughed. "But who'd imagine that stuffy Samantha Wyatt could turn out to be as good on the baseball diamond as she is in the House of Representatives? Are you coming with us for the victory celebration? Beer and pizza—that was the deal, you see. And since you're the star player..."

Samantha smiled, giving up on the dress. "In our office, we don't take time for celebrations."

"Maybe you work too hard."

"That's the way we like it."

He gave her an amused appraisal. "You've always been a workaholic, Wyatt. Always on top of things. Doesn't the Speaker let you take a break? Not even on a Friday night?"

"The Speaker lets me run the office my own way," Samantha retorted cheerfully. "If he were in charge, we'd be playing golf every afternoon."

"A golf course is sometimes a good place to do business," countered the vice president. "Why don't you come see me sometime, Miss Wyatt? I could use someone like you on my staff."

Samantha wasn't too shaken to respond to the suggestion. She was accustomed to job offers coming from unexpected places. At the moment, she was the Administrative Assistant for the Speaker of the House— essentially running Speaker Glendenning's office on Capitol Hill as well as functioning as his liaison to his local constituency. She'd been in her job for three years and loved the stimulation, the political excitement, the sheer hard work that resulted in rewards for people all over the country. She had no intention of leaving the Speaker's office. Still, it was gratifying to be asked.

"I'm happy where I am," she said, turning down the vice president's proposal with a smile. "But thanks for the offer."

He shrugged . "No harm asking. See you next game, Wyatt. And bring your friend again. He seems to have the power to throw your game off."

"My friend?"

"You know. Your boyfriend."

Boyfriend? Hardly! But Samantha found herself turning and searching the rapidly departing crowd for the man she'd knocked to the ground. Around her, the two teams were quickly dispersing as rain began to sprinkle down from above.

"Looking for these?" a voice asked.

She spun around, and there he was, towering over her, holding her shoes in one hand. He had a powerful, rangy build and weather-beaten clothes from which the rainwater seemed to run off without soaking in. Samantha could easily believe he'd just walked out of darkest Africa—he looked the type. In the getup he was wearing, he could have led safaris to the source of the Nile.

And without speaking a word, he also exuded a distracting sexual energy. It was unnerving, and Samantha hated to find herself unnerved.

But she managed to plaster a cool smile on her face. "Oh, there they are."

"You kicked them off."

"Uh, yes. Thank you."

He handed the shoes over without a fuss, and Samantha quickly tried to slip them on. She lost her balance for an instant and ended up leaning on the man's outstretched arm to hold herself upright while maneuvering her shoes onto her wet feet. She caught him watching her with a certain gleam in his eye that was unmistakable.

"You're making me feel half-naked," she said tartly, at last letting go of his arm.

"I'm sure that would be a treat," he replied with an ingenuous grin.

"Look," she said, stern but still polite, "I don't know who you are, but—"

"Then let's introduce ourselves."

"Let's not. I make it a point not to meet dangerous men."

"Are you afraid of dangerous men? Or just men in general?"

"I don't have time for men at all," she said evenly, determined not to be frightened. "So let's not allow this encounter to deteriorate into a pickup, shall we?"

"It was more of a knockdown, wasn't it?"

"See here—" she began, annoyed and starting to steam.

"I'm seeing plenty," he cut in, casting an appreciative glance down her soiled dress to the run in her stocking and back up to her necklace, which was now askew, thanks to their abrupt meeting. He reached over and used his forefinger to put the necklace back where it belonged. His touch felt like a high voltage spark on her skin. "And I like what I see very much. Look, I'm not very good at this kind of thing, but what do you say we grab a cab and have some dinner together?"

"What do you say I call the first cop I see and have you arrested?"

He laughed. "Okay, I'm probably coming on too strong. I'm out of practice. I don't know what's come over me, exactly, but—"

"You mean you're not usually such a thug?"

"I'm not a thug at all. My name's Abel Fletcher. I work at the Smithsonian."

"How nice for you," Samantha said, ignoring this offered handshake. "But we'll cut the pleasantries short, if you don't mind. I'd like to get out of this rain before I'm completely soaked. See you around."

He caught her arm in a lightning-fast grip. "Don't go. We can't part like this. I have to know how to get in touch with you."

"Why?"

"Because I—just because, that's all. This is fate. It's destiny or something. We were meant to come together like this."

Samantha lost her patience then. There were crazy people all over the city, and she had to end up talking with one while all the people who worked in her office ran for their cars. She snatched her arm from his grasp and said, "I don't know who put you up to this stunt, my friend, but the joke's over. I don't care who you are, or what you—"

"This is no joke!"

"Oh, no? You mean to say that someone didn't pay you to make a fool of me just now? Like that time they sent me one of those awful male strippers for my birthday?

"Good Lord!" She gasped, suddenly certain of what was happening. " *That's* why you're dressed in that getup! See here, if you take off one single item of clothing, I will—"

"Hey, slow down," said Abel Fletcher. "I don't know what you're talking about. I just know that I have to see you again."

Obviously he was telling the truth. Samantha restrained a sigh of relief. The birthday stripper fiasco had been the talk of Capitol Hill for weeks—and one of the most embarrassing events of Samantha's life. "Don't be absurd," she managed to say composedly. "Good night."

He followed her doggedly and managed to grab her raincoat before Samantha could lay a hand on it. "What's so absurd?" he demanded. "You're a desirable woman and I—"

"Give me my coat, please!"

As though he had suddenly remembered the rudiments of being a gentleman, he hastily held the coat open and helped her into it. Standing behind her, he asked, "You don't believe me, do you? That I could be attracted to you?"

Samantha snatched her coat around her body and spun to glare at him haughtily. "I have very firm beliefs about myself, Mr. Fletcher, and I know I'm not the desirable type, so—"

"Not desirable!" He hooted. "Lady, don't they have mirrors where you live?"

She took a deep breath and counted to ten. "Look, let's just call it a night, all right? We're both getting soaked to the skin, and I have a briefcase full of work to—oh, damn, where's my briefcase?"

He found it in a matter of seconds and brought it to Samantha as eagerly as an anxious-to-please puppy. "Here. Hell's bells, what are you carrying in this thing? Bricks?"

"My work," she snapped, grabbing the handle.

"There must be enough work in there to last you a month. Let me carry it home for you?"

"You don't expect me to lead you to my doorstep, do you?"

"I'll find out one way or another, if I have to," he said, smiling smugly. "I'll follow you home or—"

"Oh, no, you won't!" The possibility horrified Samantha.

"All right," he said calmly. "Tell me who you are and I'll be civilized. Your name is Samantha. I know that much. Now tell me the rest."

Samantha was amazed that a maniac had the guts to accost her when they were still within shouting distance of her friends. But she could see he was perfectly serious about following her home, and that seemed like a very bad idea. "I'm Samantha Wyatt," she said at least, giving in despite the voice of reason in the back of her head. "I work for the Speaker of the House."

His eyes narrowed. "Are you lying?"

"I should be, but I couldn't think of a plausible fib in time."

"I like honesty in a women. Now, where do you live?"

"I'd be a fool to tell you."

"I promise I won't lurk on your doorstep."

"You *promise*?" She gave a laugh of amazement. "All right, if you're really a psychotic ax murderer, you're not a very good one. I live in Georgetown, and that's all you're going to get."

"But I want to know—"

"No more. There are rules about talking to crazy people, and you're definitely crazy."

He grinned again. "It probably looks that way. I feel like I have to get to know you, that's all. I'm not like this normally." Then he paused, looking startled again—as though a sudden thought had occurred to him. He stared into space for a moment.

"What's the matter?" Samantha asked. "Are you going to try to tell me you haven't been yourself lately?"

In a peculiar voice, he said, "Maybe I'm *not* myself."

Oh-oh. Next he was going to start having delusions. Samantha began to edge away from him.

He didn't try to follow her. He stood there in the rain, frowning to himself, seeming truly bewildered.

Then he took something out of his pocket and stared at it. "My God, " he said. "It's working."

He didn't look dangerous anymore. He just looked confused. The rain was running off his leather jacket, soaking his hair, spattering on the little stone in his hand, but he didn't seem to notice. He had gone into a kind of trance.

Samantha decided it was time to escape, but she hesitated. "Is something wrong?"

He didn't respond.

"I hope I didn't hurt you," she said, trying again. "When I knocked you down, I mean. Are you all right?"

"I'm fine," he said, though he obviously wasn't quite sure.

Samantha cleared her throat, torn now about leaving a helpless lunatic. "If you're not feeling well I could call a cab to take you home."

He shook his head dazedly. "My car's parked nearby. Really, I'm okay."

Then he looked at her again. "You know," he said, looking almost soulful as the rain dripped off his nose, "you're very beautiful."

Samantha opened her mouth and realized she didn't have a comeback for that one.

He said, "I could stand here all night and look at you."

He was nuts! Samantha knew her hair was hanging in sodden clumps around her shoulders, there was mud caked in her shins, and she could feel her dress clinging damply to her body. But the look in his eyes made Samantha almost believe he was telling the truth.

He smiled. "Good night, Samantha."

She noticed he did not say goodbye. Turning, Samantha made a quick escape up the sidewalk past the White House, heartily thankful that Abel Fletcher remained exactly in the spot where she'd left him. She glanced back once. He watched her pensively, the rain glistening on his jacket. He didn't lift his hand to return her quick wave but stayed riveted to the ground, looking vaguely dreamy.

"Weird," Samantha muttered under her breath.

Quickly she headed across Pennsylvania Avenue to Lafayette Park and caught the first bus heading into Georgetown. Settling herself into an empty seat, Samantha looked out the window to see if she had been followed, but there was no sign of the Great White Hunter.

Normally she used the eight minute ride home to check her calendar and make a few efficient notes for tomorrow's schedule, but tonight Samantha found herself staring queerly into space and wondering about her strange encounter with Abel Fletcher. Definitely strange. Why had he picked her, of all the women around? There were much younger, sexier women to choose from. Why had she been his target?

She almost missed her stop but bounded off the bus on P Street and marched three blocks under the dripping trees to the brick townhouse she shared with Carly Moffat.

Carly—her real name was Carmel, though she didn't reveal that secret to many people—was on the telephone in the downstairs hall when Samantha let herself in. They pantomimed greetings, Carly making a pop-eyed face when she saw Samantha's wet clothes, muddy legs, and grass-stained backside.

She covered the phone receiver and said, "Hi, roomie! Taken up mud wrestling, have you?"

"Not by choice. A chance encounter with a crazy man, that's all."

"You were *mugged*?" Carly cried, alarmed.

"Nothing of the sort," Samantha assured her. "An accident, that's all—and my fault, to boot." It had been, in a way. Except that Samantha had a distinct memory of Abel Fletcher actually walking into her path as she ran for home plate. She shook off the thought and asked Carly, "Who're you talking to?"

"My mom. She's in town for the evening. She wants to take me shopping for trousseau stuff and invited you to come along for dinner. I think she's got another fish on the line for you."

"Why does everyone I know think I need a match-maker?"

"Probably because you spend eighteen hours a day with a married congressman who treats you like his daughter."

Samantha made a face. "Tell your mom I appreciate the thought, but I've got that party at the Canadian Embassy tonight. It's for the wheat lobbyists."

Carly sighed but didn't look surprised. She went back to her telephone call. "No dice, Mom. Sam's busy tonight. Something about baking bread with Canadians."

With a laugh, Samantha hustled up the stairs and headed for her room—one of three bedrooms in the small, but very high-rent townhouse she shared with Carly. Carly was the perfect roommate—she was a wonderful cook and only lived in the house on week-days, since she went home to her family's country house every weekend. Carly paid a little money toward the rent and provided just enough company to keep Samantha from going nuts by herself. Samantha wasn't looking forward to Carly's wedding—not that she wanted to deny Carly any happiness. But Samantha knew she'd never find a roommate as perfect as Carly again.

Samantha's room was at the back of the house. It was not the largest bedroom, but Samantha had selected it because of the French windows that opened onto a small balcony. Entering her bedroom was always like setting foot in a little corner of heaven. With her brutal schedule, busy office, and complicated social life, Samantha needed a place where she could relax.

Completely unlike her streamlined, no-nonsense office, the bedroom was decorated in a mishmash of her grandmother's chintz furniture and articles Samantha had picked up on her various travels—photos she'd taken herself, museum posters advertising exhibits she'd especially enjoyed, knickknacks from all over the world. Things didn't match, but what counted most to Samantha was mood. It was quiet here—soothing and cozy. The soft yellow paint Samantha had chosen for her walls enhanced the feeling that her room was always filled with sunshine.

Her cat Peaches, a fat calico she'd brought home from the animal shelter one lonely Christmas, looked up from her favorite place on the windowsill—the spot where the cat could keep her eye on the antics of the squirrels outside.

Samantha rumpled the purring cat's ears, then cast open the tall windows and leaned against the frame, breathing in the scent of the rain and flowering trees that grew in their small backyard. On the evening breeze came the restful music of wind chimes, ones Samantha had bought while on a congressional junket to China with the Speaker several years back.

Samantha sighed. She felt stirred up inside which was unusual for her after a good day's work. For once she didn't feel up to serious conversation or wheeling and dealing with lobbyists. It was all the fault of that blasted Fletcher character. He'd managed to jangle her nerves in a matter of minutes, and now she couldn't concentrate.

Grumbling, she turned back into the room and began to strip off her soiled dress. It was a mess, all right. Samantha tossed it onto a chair, making a mental note to drop it off at the dry cleaner's in the morning. Then she caught sight of herself in the antique mirror beside the closet.

Her skin looked pearly in the oblique evening light, her hair wild and—well, sexy, for heaven's sake. It was a startling sight. Samantha assumed she'd put sexiness behind her—at the age of thirty-eight, she told herself she was no longer going to submit herself to the little humiliations that went along with intimate relationships. It was easier to deal with matters of national security than with her own feelings sometimes. Men were no competition for politics.

But tonight, even Samantha couldn't miss the glow of something different in the face that stared back at her from the mirror.

I could look at you all night. That's what he'd said.

Aloud, she said, "Maybe you should have brought him home after all."

She jumped, shocked that she'd actually said the words out loud.

What was she thinking of? Had one encounter with a man rendered her silly? Worse yet, this man was obviously a mental case!

As she grabbed her robe from its hook on the bathroom door, she heard the telephone ring. A moment later, Carly called up the stairs to her.

"Sam? Phone!"

Buffing her hair with a towel, Samantha picked up the receiver of the portable telephone by her bed. It was probably Speaker Glendenning, checking last minute notes before the party. She made an effort to sound businesslike. "Yes?"

"Samantha?"

It wasn't the Speaker's voice that tingled in her ear and sent a quiver down her spine.

"It's me," he said when she didn't respond. "Abel Fletcher."

She seized the neckline of her bathrobe and hugged it close around her throat, panicked that he sounded so close. "What do you think you're doing?" she demanded, voice strangled. "How did you get this number?"

"You're in the book," he said simply. "Listen, don't be frightened, okay? I'm not stalking you or anything."

"Exactly what *are* you doing?"

"I think I just wanted to hear your voice again. You have a very unusual voice."

Samantha nearly choked. Phone calls from strange men scared the heck out of her, but knowing a screwball was on the other end of the line was even worse. "You know my address now, too, don't you?"

"Yeah," he said, and she could picture his running his finger down the phone book page to double check. "Your address is here, all right. Nice neighborhood. But that's not why I'm calling. I won't come knocking on your door."

"Are you hiding in a doorway across the street?"

"I'm not that kind of guy," he insisted. "Honest, I'm at home."

"I don't believe you."

"But—"

"I'm hanging up."

"No, wait!" he cried.

"I don't talk to strangers on the phone. And certainly not to men who follow me—"

"I haven't followed you," he said in a rush. "I'm really at home. Hold it, I'll turn on my dishwasher to prove it, okay? Can you hear that?"

The unmistakable sound of water sloshing in an appliance came over the wire, and as she listened to it, Samantha found the noise strangely reassuring. She could hear a spoon or something clunking inside the machine. Somehow she didn't picture the average psychotic killer having a loose spoon in his dishwasher.

He came back on the line. "Are you still there?"

Still suspicious, she asked, "What do you want from me, Mr. Fletcher?"

"I want you not to be scared."

"I'm not scared, I'm *angry*. I don't like being intimidated.

"I'm not trying to intimidate you. I'm—well . . ."

"Well what?"

"This sounds crazy," he said. "Believe me, I'm a perfectly sensible person under most circumstances. But I—well, something very strange has happened. If I explain, you'll think I've lost my marbles."

"I *know* you've lost your marbles."

"Please, I—didn't you feel something unusual when we met"

"All I felt was your knee between my—"

"I don't mean that," he said quickly. "It's something else. It's uncanny, but—"

"Look, Mr. Fletcher, I really do have an important appointment tonight and I haven't got much time, so—"

"With another man?"

"What?"

"Your appointment. Is it a date?"

"That's *none* of your business!"

"I have to know," he insisted, sounding desperate. "You're not married, are you?"

"No," said Samantha, thinking fast. "But I have a very big boyfriend."

Silence greeted that declaration. Then he said, "I think you're lying. That's okay, I guess. There's no reason in hell why you should trust me."

"You've got that right!"

"But you're still talking to me," he said, sounding pleased, "so you must be intrigued."

Samantha ground her teeth. All right, she was a little intrigued, but she wasn't going to admit it. "I'm being polite, that's all."

When he spoke again, she thought she could hear a smile in his low, velvety voice. He said, "I wonder if you're polite all the time?"

It was a loaded question spoken in a tone that implied something Samantha never considered. "Not so polite as to listen to suggestive remarks on the phone," she said firmly. "Look, Mr. Fletcher—"

"You're in a rush, I know. I suppose there's not much chance you'd meet me later—after your appointment? We could have a beer someplace or—"

"Absolutely not."

"Why not?"

"Why *not*? Why—" Samantha sputtered. "You—you have to admit this is a very peculiar thing you're doing."

"I know," he said, heaving a miserable sigh. "Believe me, it's not my standard operating procedure."

"You don't make a habit of stalking women, I take it?"

"Usually it's the other way around."

"I beg your pardon?"

"Women are usually all over me," he said, matter of fact. "I'm considered a very good catch. I'm not bad to look at, I'm thought to be brilliant in my field—"

"And you're modest, too, I notice."

"My point is I shouldn't be desperate to see you, but—"

"Then why are you calling?"

"I couldn't help myself! From the moment I saw you, I haven't been able to think of anything else. You're beautiful, you're smart, you're sexy! Your body makes me—"

"Slow down," Samantha warned.

"I'm serious! You're the most desirable woman I've ever met."

"Don't be ridiculous."

"You don't believe me?"

"I'm no longer young and foolish, Mr. Fletcher. I know who I am and what I am."

"And that is?"

"A woman who has her head screwed on tight."

He sighed like a lovesick teenager. "And a lovely head it is, too."

"Listen," Samantha said, patience wearing thin, "why don't you save your patter for a more appreciative audience? This city is full of silly young girls who'd love to—"

"I don't want a silly young girl. I want *you*."

"But—"

"I'm wild about you, Samantha."

"*Why?*"

"Who can explain these things? Granted, you could use some loosening up, but—"

"Loosening up?"

"Sure. You look like the tea and crumpets type, and that just won't work at all. But we'll soon fix that."

"We will, will we?"

"Yep. I'm nuts about you, Samantha. And if you don't believe me, I guess I'll just have to prove it."

"No, no," she said quickly. "You don't have to do any such thing."

"Sure I do. Wait and see. I'm going to prove you're the sexiest woman alive, Samantha Wyatt."

On that threat, he hung up, leaving Samantha listening to a dial tone and her own pounding heartbeat.

Three

___

At his apartment in Alexandria later that night, Abel stared at the stone in his hand and marveled at its power.

"It can't be possible," he muttered, turning the piece over and over. "Is a stupid little rock making me act like a dope?"

He'd seen stranger things, of course. Working for the museum had given Abel a view of a large number of peculiar artifacts that most average citizens never even dreamed of. He thought he'd seen everything. But this—it was downright scary!

Of course, he'd never behave so ridiculously if he weren't under the nefarious influence of some evil island voodoo. What sane man would be so quickly obsessed by a woman otherwise?

"I don't believe in love at first sight," he said to himself. "I don't. That's kid stuff. It's got to be this damned stone that's making me crazy."

And he *was* crazy. He couldn't get Samantha Wyatt out of his head! She was more beautiful and intelligent and witty and charming than any other female he'd ever met. And he'd been drawn to her by magic— a perfectly sane man had been seized in the grip of a force more powerful than he'd ever imagined.

Miserably he climbed into bed with a good book, hoping to forget Samantha for a while, but he found himself staring at the stone and wondering about her. Worse, he began to torment himself with the mental image of Samantha Wyatt dancing in another man's arms, chatting with someone else over glasses of wine, engaging some other guy in an intellectual discussion that showed her wit, charm, and intelligence. Was she really on a date with someone else?

To the stone, he said, "I thought the magic was supposed to work on *both* of us. She thinks I'm fresh out of a padded cell! Why isn't she falling at my feet and tearing her clothes off?"

He snapped off the light and pounded his pillow, growling with frustration. All he could think about was Samantha Wyatt—beautiful, sexy, and untouchable.

But not untouchable for long. A plan began to grow in Abel's mind. He tossed and turned all night, thinking and plotting, and when he arose on Saturday morning, he was ready.

First order of the day—sending her flowers, exactly the kind of dopey thing a woman like her ought to appreciate.

* * *

On Saturday Samantha was awakened by the florist's surly delivery man who thrust a huge box of roses into her arms before stomping back to his truck, deaf to Samantha's protests that it wasn't her birthday. Mystified, she opened the card and began to read aloud:

"'Roses are red, Your eyes are green, I'm in my bed, And you're—' —Good Lord!"

Samantha caught sight of the signature and threw the card onto the floor.

"What does that oaf think he's doing now?" she demanded, snatching open the box to discover a dozen long-stemmed roses.

"What a schmaltzy trick!" she muttered. "Does he think I'm the kind of dope who will fall for an obvious maneuver like this?"

She considered throwing the box into the street, but after a full minute of fuming in the open doorway—a full minute in which she also inhaled the exquisite fragrance of the roses—she finally closed the door and took the flowers into the kitchen. She was partial to roses, after all.

Muttering about the ignorant schemes of manipulating men, she arranged the flowers in a vase, then impulsively took one blossom upstairs to admire while she dressed.

Samantha had spent every Saturday for the past four years closeted with Speaker Glendenning at his office—arguing, theorizing, plotting. The usual. The Speaker made her jump through hoops so that by nightfall she was whipped and went to bed early, glad to have the sweet smell of the single rose to lull her into unconsciousness.

No late night phone call from Abel Fletcher disturbed her sleep. But as Samantha drifted off, she wondered dimly if she was experiencing a calm before the storm.

On Sunday morning, a refreshed Samantha dressed in a flowered, midcalf length linen skirt with a matching sweater jacket both in pale pink, not usually a color she wore to the office, since she considered pink to be frivolous. Dressed in the color of cotton candy, she looked too feminine for work, but for a party it was acceptable. On the second Sunday of every month, she was scheduled to attend a brunch given in the home of the Speaker and Mrs. Glendenning. She completed her outfit with flat shoes perfect for playing croquet on the Glendenning lawn, and a wide-brimmed straw hat to prevent freckles.

The monthly brunches were pleasant duty for Samantha. She caught a cab to the Speaker's elegant home in Bethesda and walked up the flower-lined sidewalk with pleasure. After all his years in politics, Speaker Glendenning knew how to give a party. Or rather, Marjorie Glendenning knew how. She capably managed the hundreds of details ahead of time so the Speaker could preside over the festivities like a caesar. Their Sunday brunches had become a Washington institution, and everyone in town hungered for invitations.

The parties were always relaxed. In the winter months, food was laid out informally in the Glendenning kitchen, and Marjorie herself donned an apron and cooked while a visiting foreign diplomat or high-ranking government official acted as guest of honor. Sometimes famous musicians were invited—not to play, but to mingle and enjoy themselves.

During the warmer months, a huge yellow- and white-striped tent was erected in the expansive backyard. An enormous buffet of delicacies was laid out on one long table, which was covered with a white linen cloth and sprays of flowers from the Glendenning garden. Familiar Washington faces played badminton with freshman congressmen, savvy reporters often scooped their competitors over Marjorie's famed crepes, and a president or two had been known to turn up looking for a frosty glass of orange juice. Leaders of the world's greatest nations could be seen wielding the Speaker's well-used croquet mallets.

The parties were not social occasions for Samantha—or for the Speaker, for that matter. They understood each other. There was business to be done, but they weren't supposed to *look* like they were orchestrating politics.

"Wonderful to see you, Samantha!" he greeted her in his booming voice as though they hadn't spent their Saturday embroiled in office business. He was a big, hale Irishman with a shock of white hair over a fleshy, strong-featured face.

She accepted his kiss on the cheek. The only occasions they ever permitted such shows of affection took place exactly where they were standing just then—in the cavernous foyer of the Speaker's home with Marjorie smiling by his side.

"Hello, sir," Samantha said with unfeigned affection. "Good morning, Marjorie. Your tulips look marvelous this year."

"I'm going to separate a number of bulbs in the fall, Samantha, dear. I intend to give some to you. It's time you started a hobby."

Samantha grinned. "Do tulip bulbs come with directions?"

"I'll bring them to your house myself," Marjorie said, grasping both of Samantha's hands in her own and giving her two quick kisses—one on either cheek. "I'll show you everything you need to know."

Samantha had no doubt that Marjorie was absolutely serious. The Speaker's wife was a generous, energetic woman who did not live in the shadow of her powerful husband, but liked to be involved in as many projects as she could manage—from big national charities to smaller missions like developing hobbies for people too busy to get started on their own.

Samantha laughed. "Will you hold it against me if I turn out to have a black thumb?"

"You won't," promised Marjorie. "I'm never wrong about such things. You've got a maternal side in you somewhere, Samantha. It just needs some coaxing."

Speaker Glendenning said, "She doesn't need coaxing, my dear. Samantha will know when the time is right. Run along and find some breakfast, Samantha. We've invited that nice young man from the *Post* this morning. I think he's looking for you."

Samantha pressed sociably through the crowd and found Robert Sherwood lounging in a shaded Adirondack chair in the backyard, eating a plate of bacon and eggs while two of the Speaker's English setters lay hopefully at his feet. Or foot, in Robert's case. His left leg was in a cast.

"A skiing accident," he told Samantha when she greeted him and politely inquired about his cast.

"Really?"

"No. Actually," he admitted sheepishly, "I fell down the stairs of our apartment while playing Duck,

Duck, Goose with my three-year-old. To tell the truth, I was afraid to admit it to you.''

Samantha was surprised. "You're afraid of me?''

"Sure, Glendenning's Dragon Lady is known all over—er—well,'' Robert said hastily, "that's none of my business. Shall we get started''

Samantha frowned as she sat down in the chair next to Robert, but she quickly put the moment behind her. She knew it was her job to leak a story to the press today, and the Speaker had chosen Robert for the job. Glendenning intended to kill a proposed increase in the defense budget, and a leaked story was the first step in his plan to rally support for his position. Robert took out his notebook and made a few notes as they spoke.

"Thanks, Miss Wyatt,'' Robert said when they'd finished their conversation.

"Just keep my name out of it.''

"Of course. I can't print it anyway, not the way you've worded things today. You're an old hand at this, aren't you?''

Usually Samantha considered such remarks compliments, but she felt a twinge of annoyance and pasted a cool smile on her mouth. "Let's not use the word 'old' just yet, please?''

Robert apologized laughingly. He tucked his notebook away and fed his leftovers to the delighted dogs, who had both managed to sneak their heads into his lap and had drooled all over his trousers. But the dogs weren't satisfied with the leftovers and proceeded to try to climb onto Robert and lick his face. He fought them off ineffectually, laughing and crying, "Help!'' from under two wriggling bodies.

Samantha tried to haul the dogs off Robert with little success.

From behind her, a stern voice commanded the dogs to desist, and the startled beasts immediately obeyed. Samantha turned, too, surprised by the unexpected aid.

"You!" she cried, jolted by the sight that greeted her eyes.

It was Abel Fletcher, looking tall, tanned, and rakish in rumpled khaki trousers and the same worn leather jacket as before. He'd shaved, though, which was an improvement, but he still looked like a pirate. There was no mistaking the scoundrel's gleam in his eye. He smiled coldly as he took in the tableau that Samantha and Robert made. He said, "Good morning, Samantha. Will you introduce me to your friend?"

Abel saw the surprise in Samantha's beautiful face, and his blood sang, his gut tightened, his heart nearly exploded with anticipation. She was more beautiful than he remembered—an exquisite woman with eyes like emeralds and a voice that could make the strongest man tremble. Her ankles were slim and delicate, her hips gently curving beneath her skirt. A sweater— fluffy and pink—hugged her body closely, yet demurely. She looked like a perfect English lady, but Abel knew there had to be warmth beneath her cool facade. She only needed the right man to show her the delights shared when opposite sexes attract. He nearly snatched her into his arms at that very moment.

He'd watched her talking with the guy in the cast. The sight had almost driven Abel crazy. He wanted to lunge across the patio and strangle the man who'd captured her attention. No mere mortal should receive her smiles or her touch.

The other guy struggled manfully to his feet, unsteady on his walking cast and seemingly oblivious that he was the object of Abel's anger. He put out his hand amiably. "Hello. I'm Robert Sherwood—from the *Post*."

Abel shook Sherwood's hand, reminding himself that it would be unsporting to hurl an already wounded man to the ground. "Abel Fletcher," he said, barely civil. "Would you mind if I challenged Samantha to a game of croquet?"

Sherwood smiled—very friendly and innocent. "By all means. Take my advice, though, and don't bet on the outcome. I hear Miss Wyatt's a crack croquet player."

Abel laughed stiffly, having already put his hand on Samantha's arm. He glanced down at her face and found her looking beautifully furious. "Does the Speaker know you're supplementing your income on his lawn, Samantha?"

Robert chuckled. "Oh, she's not really a hustler. But watch yourself just in case."

"Thanks for the tip." With that Abel smoothly steered her away from Robert. She hung back, but he bullied her to the edge of the patio.

"Wh—what do you think you're doing?" she demanded.

"Keep you voice down. People will think I'm kidnapping you."

"Are you?"

"I'm thinking it over," he snapped, still gripping her arm. "Who was that guy? Your boyfriend?"

She was intoxicating—green eyes throwing sparks, her mouth trembling at the edges, her whole body taut with anger. Her hair was pulled tightly back from her face, then cunningly braided down the back of her head in a style that Abel itched to loosen. Both her skirt and sweater were fastened with lots of buttons—buttons that would have to be undone one at a time.

As if guessing the direction of his thoughts, Samantha drew herself up sternly. "Robert is a professional acquaintance. You didn't have to act like a—a jealous barbarian!"

"I *am* jealous. Is he the guy you spent Friday night with? And yesterday, too?"

She succeeded in wrenching her arm from his grasp. "Who I see is none of your business. What are you doing here, anyway? This is a private party."

"I was invited."

She glared at him. "Don't try to put one over on me, Mr. Fletcher! I helped make up the guest list."

"Well, you must have missed my name. It was a late addition."

"What does that mean? Are you a legitimate guest or not?"

"Of course I am. Mrs. Glendenning invited me."

"*Mrs.* Glendenning? How on earth—"

"She's on the museum board. I called and asked if I could come."

Samantha stared at him. "And she let you in? Just like that?"

He smiled. "I can be very persuasive."

Samantha looked thoroughly steamed. Abel wasn't surprised, but he figured she was going to get over the angry phase soon enough. He had a plan, and he intended to see it through. Because of the stone, he wanted this woman badly—more than he'd ever wanted anyone before. And Abel was not a man to ignore his desires.

The English setters stood at attention, side by side at Abel's heels, gazing up at him adoringly. He ignored them, but the dogs behaved as if he was their lord and master. With a single command, he had enslaved them. It was a knack he'd always had, but he knew the sight infuriated Samantha.

She glared at the dogs. "Go away," she snapped, swishing her be-ribboned hat at them. "Shoo!"

Neither moved a muscle.

Abel's smile broadened. "I'm demonstrating my magnetic personality."

"I see that animals find you highly magnetic. But I, on the other hand—"

"You'll come around. You look delicious today, Samantha. You don't know how badly I want to kiss you."

Alarmed, she backed up several paces until she collided with a maple tree. She composed herself and lectured him. "Mr. Fletcher, from this moment onward, you are never going to manhandle me again. Do you understand? I will not be dragged or kissed or have my arm nearly broken by—"

"You're absolutely right. I've behaved unforgivably, and I should be sorry, but I'm not. Look, everybody's starting to wonder what we're arguing about. Let's play croquet and put the Speaker's guests at ease."

Samantha glanced sharply around and must have seen that he was right. People *were* turning to watch the two of them, but Abel noticed that nobody was running to her rescue. Rather, most of the guests seemed to be smiling in Samantha's direction.

"They think we're lovers," Abel murmured in her ear.

Samantha spun to face him, but kept her voice down this time. "I am not your lover! Nor am I *going* to be your lover! For heaven's sake, I don't even *like* you very much! Who *are* you?''

She was intoxicating. Passion beat close to the surface of her ladylike disguise. The unusual timbre of her voice again caused a visceral reaction in Abel. Overcome by her proximity, he said, ''I've never seen eyes as beautiful as yours. And the sunlight on your hair makes me—''

''Stop that!'' She looked mortified.

''I can't help it,'' he said, following her. ''You're the most wonderful woman I've ever met.''

''But we *haven't* met! I don't know you! You're a lunatic!''

He caught her hand in his, taking care to be gentle this time. The next step was putting her at ease—showing Samantha that he could be trusted. ''All right, all right. I'll tell you everything about myself while we play. I'm not a criminal, honest.''

She extricated her hand firmly. ''I'm more worried that you're some kind of sex maniac.''

He grinned. ''Would that be so bad?''

Her eyes flew wide open. ''Get away from me!''

''I can't. I'm bewitched. I want to follow you everywhere—to the ends of the earth, if I have to.'' He bent, picking up two mallets from the grass. Then, staying on one knee, he coaxed her with all the charm he could muster. ''Play croquet with me, Samantha. With all these people around, you'll be perfectly safe. Please?''

Her face turned pink. ''Get up, for heaven's sake!''

Their hushed argument had drawn the attention of the Speaker's guests, and Samantha was thoroughly flustered. She weighed the situation rapidly, though, and Abel could see that she'd have plenty of explaining to do if she made a dramatic exit and left him there on bended knee.

So she managed a false smile for the benefit of their audience, a smile that did not reach her eyes. From between gritted teeth, she said, "I will play one *short* game on the condition that you get up at once and tell me exactly who you are and how you gate-crashed this party."

"I did not gate-crash," Abel corrected, obeying her command to stand up.

He slipped his hand smoothly under her elbow as they crossed the lawn to the first wicket. The dogs followed him like twin shadows. "I spent all day yesterday learning about you, and my superior at the museum mentioned this party. He offered his invitation, generous fellow that he is, so I took it. At least, I understood it that way. Leaving the card in plain view on his desk is just asking to have it stolen, right?"

"You *stole*—"

"Anyway, I phoned Mrs. Glendenning to be sure it was okay if I came in his place. She was charmed."

"I can see why you used the telephone. One look at you would have changed Marjorie's mind, I'm sure."

"What's wrong with the way I look?"

She cast a derisive glance down his jacket and trousers, "You can hardly claim to fit in at this party, can you? People are staring."

"As long as you're staring, too, I'm happy."

"Look—"

"I'm not a shirt and tie man, Samantha," he told her firmly. "But that's okay. You're ready for a change."

Samantha shot him a fiery look, then lifted her nose and put her hat on her head, refusing to respond.

While primly tying the bow under her chin, she explained the game of croquet in stern tones. Abel barely listened to her words. He was enraptured, enjoying the sound of her voice, the flash of her eyes, the easy grace of her body as she tapped her ball into play.

He also enjoyed watching her hips move under her skirt as she made her way to the first wicket. He liked her natural swing, her keenly focused attention. He noticed how her lipstick had been precisely applied—a soft color that matched her sweater. Abel hungered to mess up that perfect pink lipstick, to tear off her perfect hat and run his fingers into her perfect hair.

She hit her ball again, and it wobbled uncertainly across the grass and came to rest in an inconvenient spot. Irritated, Samantha glared at it. Abel longed to kiss the little frown between her fine brows. The stone's magic was working stronger than ever this morning.

But he prevented himself from kissing Samantha and instead eyed her position bemusedly. "Do you suppose we should make a friendly wager on this contest, after all?"

"Don't let my first shot make you cocky," she said defensively. "I'm very good at this game."

"Then you won't mind making a bet, right?"

She blinked, suddenly looking as provocatively innocent as Scarlett O'Hara under the brim of her hat. In that moment, Abel wondered if he was looking at a killer card player. She said, "I'm not carrying much cash—only enough cab fare to get home."

He grinned, guessing that she was bluffing. "Let's not be so uncouth as to use cash, my dear Miss Wyatt. We can be more sporting than that."

Suspiciously, Samantha said, "How sporting?"

He hit his own ball—a surprisingly good shot—and leaned on his mallet. "I suppose kisses are out of the question?"

"Absolutely."

"How about dinner tonight? I know a great place for mesquite hamburgers."

"Impossible. I've got a meeting."

"Come now, Samantha, is Glendenning's Dragon Lady really as hardworking as they say she is?"

Her spine straightened with a snap. "Who called me that abominable name?"

"Everybody! You're the Terror of the Tidal Basin, too. Do you realize you've got most of Washington browbeaten?"

"I get the job done," she snapped tartly. "Anyway, I haven't intimidated everyone in Washington. *You* seem to be pretty calm."

"That's because I know what's underneath that prissy act of yours, Samantha."

Her face closed up at once. "I'll thank you not to make assumptions about me, Mr. Fletcher. If I have a tough reputation, I'm proud it it, and I plan to keep on doing it well for a long time to come."

"But all work and no play..."

"Oh, I play," said Samantha. She whacked her ball, succeeding in making a tricky shot that dashed through the next wicket. She gave Abel a sparkling smile of triumph. "Sometimes I play very well."

He was glad to see her fear and anger fading. The loveliness of the smile she gave him was like an arrow sinking deep into his heart. But he forced himself to say lightly, "Do you play other games as well?"

"Don't challenge me, Mr. Fletcher," she warned, just as lightly, "unless you don't mind losing."

There was no time for a snappy comeback to that. They were interrupted by the arrival of Speaker Glendenning, who carried a glass of mimosa in one hand and fanned his florid face with a straw boater. "Samantha!" he called. "Introduce me to your friend!"

"He isn't my friend," Samantha said calmly. "He's the crazy man I was telling you about yesterday. Mr. Speaker, this is Abel Fletcher."

"Fletcher!" The Speaker seized Abel's hand and pumped it vigorously, laughing loudly. "You're hot in pursuit of our fair Samantha, are you?"

"I'm trying, sir."

"Has she thanked you for the roses yet?"

"No, sir, I assumed she threw them away."

The Speaker cocked a bushy white brow at Samantha. "Well, young lady?"

Samantha looked uncomfortable but recovered quickly. "I did not throw them away," she said sedately. "Thank you for the flowers, Mr. Fletcher. They're beautiful."

But the tiny flicker in Samantha's eyes told him that she had seen through the flowers ploy. Abel had underestimated her intelligence and vowed to be more careful in the future. He said, "Beautiful roses for a beautiful lady."

The Speaker roared with laughter. "You'll never get anywhere with her if you pussyfoot around like this, Fletcher. Come now! I hear you're a man of action. Take matters into your own hands!"

"Count on it," Abel replied.

The Speaker grinned. "Good. You know, we're all rooting for you, my boy. It's time Samantha stopped seeing those milquetoast types she usually brings around."

Abel laughed—mostly at Samantha's appalled expression. "Thank you, sir. I'm delighted to have your approval."

Glendenning continued to speak in his booming, statesman's voice. "Marjorie tells me you come from the Smithsonian."

"The Air and Space Museum, to be exact, sir. I'm a field curator."

"Oh? What does that mean exactly?"

"I travel around digging up old airplanes, mostly. Then I bring them here to our restoration facility in Suitland, Maryland, and supervise their reconstruction."

"You're a pilot, too?"

"Of course."

"Well, perhaps you can cure Miss Wyatt of her fear in that department."

Abel turned an amused and inquiring glance down at Samantha.

Clearly hating having her weakness exposed, she started, "Sir, I don't think you need to—"

But Glendenning waved her protests away. "Samantha's a perfect employee in every way but one—we have to drag her onto airplanes. Otherwise, she's topnotch. I hear you're no slouch at your work either, Fletcher. Your bosses say you're the best."

Abel endeavored to look modest. "My colleagues tell me I've just managed to find a job that lets me collect the biggest toys in the world."

The Speaker laughed appreciatively. "Perhaps you'll give me a tour one of these days. I'd love to see your toys."

"I'd be honored."

The Speaker turned to Samantha. "Well, my dear, I don't think you have anything to fear from Abel. He comes highly recommended, Marjorie tells me. She checked him out thoroughly. He's relatively upstanding, if a little unorthodox. And I like him. He's got—" The Speaker sought a word that was suitable for the company of ladies. "He's got gumption!"

Composedly, Samantha said, "Why doesn't that make me feel better?"

Glendenning laughed and made light conversation for a few minutes. During that time Abel decided he was a true old-style politico—a man who had devoted his life to public service and loved every minute of it. He had a big, brassy personality but a keen eye for detail. Abel suspected that behind the seemingly innocent questions, the Speaker was sizing him up. That meant he truly cared for Samantha, which made Abel feel like a prospective son-in-law being interviewed by the father of the bride. He did his best to make a good impression, but his mind was distracted. All he could think about was the beautiful woman at his side—and how much he wanted to be alone with her.

He knew the Speaker saw exactly what he was feeling. There was a twinkle in the old man's eye.

Glendenning clapped Abel on his shoulder. "Well, my boy, I'll call you about that tour soon. I won't forget, you know."

Abel doubted that the Speaker ever forgot any promise. The man was no doubt a formidable opponent in a fight. "I'll be waiting, sir."

"Samantha," Glendenning said, lecturing, "don't take this boy lightly. I think he's the fellow who could turn your life upside down."

"I prefer my life right side up," she replied.

Abel couldn't help saying, "Life without surprises is boring."

"Boring can be very pleasant," she retorted, giving him a look that could melt an ice floe."

The Speaker laughed at her. "How can any intelligent woman think sex is boring?"

Abel said, "Maybe she's just been doing it wrong."

Samantha looked mortified. Glendenning roared until the tears came, then whistled to his dogs and staggered off, leaving them alone.

Samantha swung on Abel furiously. "How could you humiliate me like that?"

"Humiliate you? Samantha, your boss knows you better than you think. I didn't say a thing that surprised him."

"I have a reputation to consider!"

"It's a damned dull reputation, if you ask me. But don't worry, we'll jazz things up. Come on, let's play."

He steered her back to the game, and Samantha couldn't protest without drawing attention to them. Abel noticed that the crowd was beginning to thin out. All he had to do was keep her distracted, and they'd soon have the backyard to themselves.

Making conversation, he said, "Glendenning seems genuinely fond of you."

"We're old friends," Samantha said, trying to line up her next shot with care. "My father was the Speaker's law partner for many years before Mr. Glendenning was elected to the House. I started working in his office as a typist when I was fresh out of college."

"And you've been there ever since?"

She tapped her ball and straightened to watch it skitter across the grass to exactly the spot she was aiming for. "For sixteen years, yes. I couldn't ask for a more exciting job."

"Most people find their excitement outside their jobs."

She cast an oblique look at him. "Not me."

Abel had to admit that he found his excitement in his work, too. Until now. At the moment, all he could think about was the outwardly self-reliant, but obviously shy and sexy woman beside him. Casually, he said, "You work twenty-four hours a day, is that it?"

"Of course not. I have outside interests."

"Like what?"

"I thought we were going to learn about *you* during this game."

He leaned on his mallet. "What do you want to know?"

For an instant, he thought she was going to refuse his offer. But she returned his gaze through narrowed eyes, and Abel wondered what she was thinking about. A fine pink blush rose in her cheeks, but she fought it down and finally said, "I suppose you think you're the original macho man."

He grinned ingenuously. "Sure do."

"And you're completely unaware that you're a decade out of date."

"What do you mean?"

"Tough guys in jungle gear are out of fashion, Mr. Fletcher. The average woman wants something else."

"But you're not an average woman, are you?"

She cracked her ball again, and it skittered through the next wicket. "No, I'm not. I've learned all I want to know about men, Mr. Fletcher. Maybe I don't look like it, but I've had a few relationships along the way.

Nothing you can say or do will interest me in trying those dangerous waters again."

While she watched her ball roll, Abel nudged his with his foot into a better position. "What's the matter?" he asked innocently. "Did you have a bad experience?"

"Let's just say I now have different priorities than most women. I didn't get where I am today by stroking a man's ego or letting him call the shots."

"There are rude names for women like that."

She picked a few blades of grass off the head of her mallet and ignored his remark. "You mentioned games before. Well, I'm finished with silly behavior like that. I don't let a man win because it will make him like me. I play to win."

"I wouldn't be here if I wasn't looking for a fair contest."

"Trouble is, women don't win the kind of contest you're trying to start with me."

Abel hit his ball. "Not ever?"

"Not often enough."

"So you avoid the risk by refusing to put yourself in a vulnerable position to start with."

"Exactly." She cracked her ball hard. The gleam of triumph shone in her eyes again as the ball rolled to a tantalizing spot just inches from the stake.

While she watched it roll smoothly to a stop, Abel kicked his own ball again. "You like to be in control all the time, don't you? Even in your love life."

"I haven't got a love life," she said at once, then looked as if she regretted the words. Giving him a cold smile, she said, "You see, Mr. Fletcher, I've learned that love makes people stupid."

He laughed. "There's freedom in stupidity, you know."

It was his turn again, so Abel took his time to calculate his shot. He hit his ball and sent it like a torpedo—straight into her ball, which then skittered sideways and disappeared under a flowering bush.

Samantha's smile disappeared. "You rat!"

"That was a fair shot."

"It was not! How did your ball get there?"

Pleased that she hadn't seen his subversive maneuver, he taunted, "You should have been paying attention to the game, Samantha."

"I was! You cheated."

Abel would rather be boiled in oil than allow a woman to beat him at any sport—even one as wimpy as croquet. So naturally he cheated. But he made a good show of looking outraged at her accusation. "You accuse *me* of cheating?"

"It would be just like a man of your type to do something underhanded!"

"I think your mind was wandering, that's all. What's the matter, Samantha?"

"Look here—"

"I'm looking," Abel said, dropping his mallet on the grass. "And I see a beautiful woman who's wrapped herself up in her work so thoroughly that she no longer sees what she missing."

"If you're about to suggest that *you* are an alternative to my sheltered existence," she retorted, with a cool laugh, "you might as well save your breath."

Abel grinned. "Why? Why not me, Samantha? I think we could be good together."

She shook her head, smiling just a little. "Oh, no, you're far too much trouble! You look like a pirate and act like some kind of crazy man—"

"What's crazy about sending flowers to a woman?"

"Your motive for sending those roses was purely self-serving, Mr. Fletcher. If you really knew me, you'd never have tried such a transparent trick."

"I *do* know you." He got closer, sliding his hand up her softly sweatered arm. The other guests had gone away, leaving the two of them alone under the shady trees. "I know everything about you, Samantha. Everything I need to know, that is. I find you very desirable despite the way you try to hide it."

She pulled away from his touch. "I'm not hiding anything."

"You're hiding your sexiness under all these prim and proper clothes." He tweaked the collar of her blouse. "Admit it. Trouble is, you've missed the point. A girl in a bikini can be sexy. But a woman like you with all her careful clothes and her proper ways... you're erotic."

With a sharply intelligent expression in her green eyes, she gazed piercingly at him. "You see me as a challenge, don't you?"

"No, you're the woman of my dreams."

She laughed brusquely. "Now I know your game! You picked me to chase around the maypole because I'd be tough to catch, right? You figure I'll be good sport for a while, but deep down inside you're assuming you *won't* catch me."

"What's that supposed to mean, Dr. Freud?"

"Men like you are drawn to women like me." She lifted her sharp, stubborn chin. "You only pursue us because you think we won't let ourselves be caught. I won't be talking about marriage and children in a few weeks, because I've got a full life already and you're safe from that old trap. Well, I haven't got time to play fox and hare right now, so you can—''

"You've got me all wrong," Abel interrupted, suddenly grasping the end of her mallet. For an instant, they both tugged on the stick, Samantha with her face tightly controlled as it tilted up to his. "You don't understand at all, Samantha. I *intend* to talk about marriage."

"What do you mean?"

"A big wedding, a long honeymoon, lots of kids someday—the whole bit."

Her confused expression grew more alarmed. "What are you babbling about?"

"I'm the man you're going to marry, Samantha Wyatt."

Her reserve broke. "You've got nerve!"

"You bet." He pulled her closer until the mallet was the only obstacle between them. "I'm the one who's going to make your life complete."

"Wait," she said, pressing one hand against his chest.

Too late. He threw the mallet aside and snared her narrow waist with one arm. In another swift motion, he pulled on the bow under her chin and removed her hat, tossing it on the grass. In the next instant, Samantha's slender body was tight against his harder frame. He could feel her breasts and her heart beating fast beneath them. In her eyes, he saw a flurry of emotions—and one flicker of willingness.

She tried to pull back. But not too hard. She *was* attracted to him! She didn't fight Abel at once, just took a second to absorb everything. No doubt she could feel his pulse, not to mention the unmistakable pressure of his arousal growing between them. Her green eyes widened, very clear in the sunlight.

Sounding shaken, she said, "This is crazy."

"You feel it, too?" he whispered, excitement growing inside.

"I don't *know* you!"

"But you want to kiss me anyway."

She was fighting herself, battling her own willpower. "Mr. Fletcher—"

"I'm Abel. Say it."

"Abel," she whispered, "I—"

"You want me to kiss you?"

"Oh, damn," she said, unsteady and weakening rapidly. She closed her eyes. "Damn everything. Let's get it over with."

"Over with?"

"Let's do it," she said, fierce suddenly. Her eyes flashed. "Go on, do it! Then we can forget about it."

He laughed. "My beautiful Samantha, this is one kiss you'll never forget."

He meant to kiss slowly, brushing her perfect mouth and coaxing with gentleness, but that plan fell apart immediately. Her lips were soft and wonderfully pliant. Abel rushed to part them and found the inside of her mouth with his tongue. She tasted hot and liquid, sweet as honey. He groaned, circling her mouth, coaxing, teasing her senses until her whole body seemed to melt and come alive in his arms.

She didn't pull away but began to tremble, breathing little quivering breaths. Abel gathered her hard against himself, longing to be closer still, inside her, a part of her. He broke the kiss, gasping for air, trying to collect his wits.

"Stop," she said, quivering as she lifted her gaze to his face and flinched at what she saw there. "This is ridiculous."

"No, it's wonderful."

He found her lips again, and this time his mind filled with erotic images of the two of them together. He wanted to feel Samantha's touch everywhere—her gentle fingertips teasing him to the edge of control. She was vibrant and vulnerable at the same time—controlled, but reckless, too. He sensed the tremble in her limbs was excitement, not fear.

He found her ear with his teeth, nuzzled her throat, blew kisses along the nape of her neck. His voice rasped with impatience. "I want to take you home to my bed, Samantha. I want to drive you out of your mind."

She met his lips the third time, no longer struggling to free herself. He kissed her long and hard, exploring, dipping into the well of her sensuality and struggling to hang onto his own composure. Without thinking, he smoothed his hand down her spine, learning every curve, every pulse point. When she arched her back, he realized he had clasped her bottom and lifted her against himself. In another moment, he was going to start unfastening all those lovely buttons and pull her down on the grass.

He started at the top of her blouse.

But she stopped him. She pushed his hand away but couldn't look him in the face. Her cheeks were flushed. Her hair had begun to escape its braid.

"Wait," she said. "I must be out of my mind."

"Feels good, doesn't it? I can make you feel even better, Samantha."

Extricating herself form his embrace, she said firmly, "That's enough. Somebody will see us, or—"

"Everybody's gone," He held her hand to keep one last connection between them. Urgently he said, "Come home with me."

"No!" Samantha faced him forcefully. "I am not going to drop everything for an afternoon of sexual delights with a man I hardly—"

"Dear Lord, let's not go through that again!"

She laughed—a little drunkenly, perhaps, but it was a laugh nevertheless. "But I *don't* know you. Oh, there must be something in the air that's made us both nuts. I'm sorry I let you kiss me. I'm sorry I kissed you back. But—"

"Can you deny there's a powerful sexual attraction between us?"

"In this town, we say 'no comment' to questions like that! Please, Mr. Fletcher. Respect my wishes on this."

"What are your wishes?" Abel demanded. "A moment ago, I thought you were wishing the same thing I was. You were ready and willing. I could feel it. Take a chance!"

"I don't take chances like this. Let me go, please."

"All right," he said, releasing her hand. "But I'm not finished. And neither are you. Tonight you're going to dream about me."

She surprised him then. With a wry smile, she said, "I dreamed about you last night."

Four

Samantha was all thumbs after the Glendenning party. She shut her foot in the door of the cab, dropped a bottle of mineral water on her kitchen floor, and smeared toothpaste on her face to remove her makeup that night.

"Normally I'm the epitome of cool, calm, and collected!" she muttered after spilling an entire cup of herbal tea all over her desk on Monday morning. "So how come I'm suddenly a moron?"

There was only one answer, and Samantha was so appalled by the idea that she refused to consider it.

"What's the matter with you?" the Speaker finally demanded.

They were in a cab headed for a Washington hotel for photographs and a reception conducted by environmental lobbyists. The cab rocketed up M Street as though it was being chased by a mob of unhappy voters waving placards. The driver looked utterly bored as the speedometer crept steadily upward. In the back seat of the jouncing vehicle, Samantha held on for dear life, but as always, Glendenning seemed unaffected by the wild ride. He could weather a hurricane without blinking an eye.

"You're a thousand miles away," complained the Speaker. "I'm venting my disgust for the terrible food they serve at these environmentalist things, and you're looking dreamy-eyed."

Samantha pulled herself together . "I'm sorry, sir. What were you saying?"

"I was saying their food always looks like seaweed."

"It probably *is* seaweed."

"What about the little orange bits of stuff?"

"Safer not to ask, sir. It might actually be good for you."

Speaker Glendenning shuddered at the thought, and Samantha relaxed and laughed. She had come to love the Speaker almost as much as her own father. He could tell a raunchy story one minute and weep over a sick baby the next. He had climbed to his current position of power by hard work and savvy politics—getting on the telephone to his cronies when he needed to rally support for legislation, doing favors for his friends, and calling in those favors when he needed them back. He was a man of his word, a man of the people, a man Samantha truly respected.

"There is honor in government service, Samantha," he had told her years ago. And she'd believed him. She still did. Working for the Speaker was rewarding in many ways. It paid pretty well, of course, and as she'd grown into her present job, there was the heady notion that she had become a power broker, one of the many invaluable cogs in the great wheel of government. But most important was Samantha's feeling that she went home every night having truly served the people of her country. In a single day, she might do some good for AIDS patients, senior citizens, or homeless children.

But now and then she wished she didn't work for such a sharp-eyed boss.

"You're thinking about young Fletcher, aren't you?" he asked suddenly, proving once again that he was nearly clairvoyant when it came to his staff.

She controlled her expression with an effort, determined not to let him guess what was on her mind. "Fletcher who?"

Glendenning laughed. "I saw you kissing in my backyard yesterday. You've got quiet a good technique, by the way. Up on tiptoes and everything, just like the movies."

Samantha felt her face get hot—embarrassed by her own behavior as much as having been caught. "Aren't there laws against voyeurism?"

With a chuckle, he said, "I didn't watch for long. Did you spend the afternoon together?"

"With a man like him? *Me*?"

"Why not?"

"Mr. Speaker," Samantha said deliberately, "a person like Abel Fletcher probably eats most of his meals out of disposable containers. He's not the man of my dreams."

"Then you're having the wrong kind of dreams my girl. *Did* you spend the afternoon with him?"

"Certainly not. I had things to do," Samantha lied. She had barely escaped the Glendenning party with her virtue. Abel Fletcher was a determined man, and she'd had a very difficult time convincing him he couldn't accompany her home.

"How about last night?" The Speaker pressed. "Sleep with him?"

Affronted, Samantha cried, "Of course not!"

The Speaker was unabashed. "Well, did he send more flowers today?"

"No," Samantha said, with less force. "This morning it was a picnic basket."

"A what?"

"He had a picnic basket delivered to my place! With caviar and wine and—and everything needed for a perfect seduction. At least, that's what his note said."

Samantha still couldn't believe how hard Abel was pushing to get to know her better. She had tried every possible way of discouraging him, but nothing seemed to work. He was a new experience for her—a man who wouldn't take Samantha Wyatt's "no" for an answer.

Grinning, the Speaker said, "He's a determined scoundrel, isn't he?"

"I think he's a fruitcake. Really, I do!" Samantha turned to the Speaker appealingly. "He's unstoppable! What could possibly cause a man to act this way?"

With a softening smile, Glendenning said, "You underestimate yourself, my dear. You're very easy on the eyes."

Samantha frowned. "He says he likes the way I look, but it's got to be more than that. I'm no Grace Kelly."

"It's called sex, honey. Haven't you heard of it yet?"

"It's more than sex, if you can believe that! He—he acts like we already know each other—as if we're connected somehow. Honestly, he's like a man possessed! It's—well, it's downright scary."

"Scary? Or exciting?"

She shot him a look. "What do you mean?"

Glendenning sighed. "Samantha, honey, we've been together a long time, you and I. I don't interfere with your life, if I can help it, but—well, I'd like to see you happy."

"I *am* happy."

"Not just ordinarily happy. I mean deliriously in love and *happy*. Let me tell you a story. When I was a young man, having a family was the last thing on my mind. I thought I had more important things on my horizon, and women were just a nice decoration at parties. Then I met Marjorie. I thought she was pretty and all, but it was Margie who decided we were meant for each other. She chased me until I was too tired to run anymore. And I'm glad she did. It sounds trite, but my life's complete now—I've got the best job in the country, the smartest, most beautiful children, and a wife who's not afraid to tell me when I'm being a pompous ass. Sometimes I look at her lovely face on the pillow at night and wonder what I would have turned out to be without her, and I—well, I'm not ashamed to admit that I get choked up at the thought."

"What are you saying, sir?"

"That maybe this Fletcher fellow is exactly what you need—a man who's tougher than you are, a man who's determined to make a *woman* out of you."

"Don't insult me, please. I'm a woman already."

"You're right. I'm sorry." Glendenning reached for her hand and gave Samantha a fatherly pat. "It's just that he could be perfect for you—a big, brawny guy with more muscles than brains—"

"He's not brainless!" Samantha stopped herself, realizing she was defending a man she was a long way from trusting. She sighed. "I can't help thinking he's got something else on his mind, though."

"Besides sex?"

Blushing again, Samantha said, "Yes."

Cocking an eyebrow, he remarked, "Suspicious, aren't we?"

"You taught me that. Politics and love affairs don't mix."

"Samantha, every man who compliments you isn't necessarily looking for a handout."

"But I did some reading this morning and discovered that there' s a bill coming up soon—one that deals with funding for museums."

"You think he's trying to influence you?"

"It's happened before. And Fletcher is—well, he—"

"He comes on strong?"

"Like a tiger in mating season!"

"So what's wrong with that? You're a grown woman. It's time you had a good hard—er—fling. And Fletcher's the man for my money."

The Speaker grew serious then, putting on his Elder Statesman expression and deepening his voice. "But you can't get completely carried away, of course. Not in this day and age. You do know about safe sex, don't you?"

The cab driver's wide eyes appeared in the rearview mirror. Samantha suppressed a humiliated groan, but there was no stopping the Speaker when he got to filibustering.

"It's important to take care of yourself," the Speaker lectured on, unaware of her embarrassment. "Responsibility is the key issue. There's no shame for a young woman to carry her own condoms these days.

It's better to be safe than sorry. I hear some ladies carry different brands in their handbags so that—''

"*Please*, sir! Can we drop this subject? I'm not going to bed with Abel Fletcher!''

"Hmm,'' said the Speaker, sounding doubtful. "Does he believe that?''

Samantha swallowed. "I don't think so.''

"Ah,'' said the Speaker, and he smiled in silence for the rest of the ride.

The lobbyist reception was a crashing bore. Samantha drank her mineral water, nibbled some tasteless canapés, and tried to make conversation with people she saw on a regular basis but with whom she seemed to have little in common. She ended up standing alone, watching the party and wondering what a man like Abel Fletcher would say about the event.

He probably wouldn't say anything. He was the type who'd swing on a vine through an open window, looking dashing in his leather jacket, and snatch up the woman of his choice before leaping over the nearest balcony for a fast getaway.

Samantha found herself smiling at the thought. She wouldn't mind a fast getaway at the moment.

But she ended up taking a bus straight home after the party with a plan to put Abel Fletcher out of her mind by reading back issues of the *Congressional Record*.

No such luck. He was sitting on the steps of her townhouse in a patch of fading sunlight that filtered through the tree branches overhead.

"Hi,'' he said when she came up the sidewalk. "Remember me?''

"How could I forget?'' Samantha's heart started pounding at the first sight of him. The memory of the way he'd kissed her had kept Samantha awake all night. One look at him, and she could almost feel the rough texture of his cheek against hers.

He got to his feet lazily, looking like a wolf awakening from a refreshing nap. His smile was crooked, his gaze hungry. Right away, Samantha felt that if he could wrap her in those smoldering dark eyes of his, she'd never need a coat again.

Instead of his leather jacket, he had on a pair of faded running shorts, worn sneakers, and a Dartmouth sweatshirt that was stretched tight across his shoulders and chest.

He caught her looking and said, "I'm dressed wrong again, am I?"

"I was just wondering what happened to your flight jacket."

"I finally unpacked from my trip and sent everything to the dry cleaner's. The jacket smelled like jungle."

"Is *that* what jungle smells like?"

He grinned and took no offense. "If you like the jacket so much, I'll call the cleaner and ask him to speed it up."

"No need for that." Samantha halted at the bottom of the steps, folded her arms and tapped her foot. "You said you weren't going to lurk on my doorstep."

"I'm not lurking, I'm standing here in broad daylight." He spread his arms and attempted to look innocent.

Samantha didn't believe his act for a second. "Why in blazes are you here, Fletcher?"

"We progressed to first names last time remember?"

"Yes. I also remember that I made myself clear concerning—"

"Oh, you were very clear. I'm just not listening. Besides, your eyes are sending a different message." Bending closer, he said, "I missed you, Samantha."

He kissed her lightly—before she could draw away—brushing his mouth across hers with a possessive air. Samantha caught a hint of his scent—clean and male. His dark hair had just enough curl to coax a woman's fingertips. And there was no ignoring that body of his—narrow hips, long legs, wonderful shoulders. He was splendid. The shirt sleeves pushed up around his elbows revealed strong, suntanned forearms, and his short shorts showed off his long, muscled legs. Even his throat, showing from the stretched-out collar of his shirt, looked dashingly virile. Samantha found herself feeling light-headed and blinking—not from the kiss, but from the sight of him standing on her front steps big as life. He was one breathtaking specimen of male anatomy, all right.

Looking into her eyes, he must have seen exactly what she was thinking, for he grinned and dropped his voice to an intimate murmur to say, "Why don't we go for a walk or something?"

"Surely a walk is too tame an amusement for the likes of you."

"You have another idea?" His eyes were almost twinkling.

An idea dawned, and Samantha said, "Why don't we go running instead"

"Running?" Abel's expression changed.

"Why not? You're dressed for it. Of course, if you're afraid I might be better than you are—"

"Are you still mad about being beaten at croquet?"

"I wasn't beaten," Samantha said tartly. "You cheated. In any case, running is one sport where you can't cheat."

Abel looked wicked. "I might come up with something. Does a woman like you go jogging often?"

"Not jogging," Samantha corrected. "I go running."

He shrugged. "Okay, I'm willing. But if you get too far behind me—"

Samantha laughed at that and poked him in the chest. "You've got a surprise coming, buster!"

He grinned lasciviously. "I hope so."

Samantha couldn't help but notice as Abel looked her up and down with an appreciative gleam in his gaze. She had worn an oversize plum-colored jacket over a black skirt, black stockings and high-heeled shoes—a kind of uniform among professional women lately. At the moment, she regretted the shortness of her skirt, though. Abel seemed beguiled by the sight of her legs.

She eyed him back and decided that even though he was in terrific physical condition, he was not built like a runner. "If I invite you inside, will I have to keep my can of Mace handy?"

He touched a wisp of her hair as it brushed her shoulder. "Let's put it this way— I won't try anything unless I'm sure you'll love it."

"Am I supposed to be relieved to hear that?"

The grin on his striking face looked positively devilish. "Would you be happier if I carried you up the stairs like Rhett Butler?"

How did he know that was her favorite scene in the movies? Samantha masked her reaction at once. She had a notion that if she let Abel know she was feeling

the slightest bit weak, he'd have her upstairs and between the sheets in ten seconds flat.

"Come on," he coaxed. "You're not still nervous,
are you? Afraid to be alone with me?"

"Of course not," she huffed. "I can take care of
myself." Snatching her keys out of her handbag, she
breezed past him and up the steps, making her decision. "Come in while I change."

She wouldn't have invited him inside if she hadn't
been darn sure her roommate was at home, of course.
But Samantha had seen Carly's compact car parked on
the street and knew help was available somewhere on
the premises, should the need arise.

"This is your house?" Abel asked when they were
inside the elegant brick townhouse. He looked around
with interest.

"I don't own it. Not yet, at least. It belongs to the
woman who was just appointed ambassador to In-
dia."

"Nice work if you can get it."

Samantha tossed her keys and bag on the table in the
entry hall and faced him. "She probably won't come
back to Washington even when her term is over. I hope
to scrape up enough cash to buy the place from her."

Abel looked down at her, amused. "Are you a real
estate tycoon, Samantha? I had you figured for the
savings account type—cautious when it comes to your
money."

"My financial portfolio, if you must know, is quite
diverse."

"So you do take risks now and then?"

"Are we talking about money? Or something else?"

"Let's call it life in general. Is the lady a gambler,
after all?"

"Only when I know the odds. I like to study the situation before I take a plunge."

His smile curved tantalizingly close. "How much studying is enough?"

Getting brave, she said lightly, "I'll let you know."

Composed despite the way her heart was banging against her ribs, Samantha showed him through the hallway into a long, handsome living room that was not furnished with the expensive, traditional furniture that usually decorated such stately houses. Samantha and Carly had combined their collected bits and pieces to make a comfortable room. A pair of white sofas belonged to Samantha, the Shaker-style tables were Carly's. Some woven wall hangings had been donated by Samantha's cousin Kate, an artist, and Carly's mother had sprung for some expensive Chinese lamps. A certain amount of clutter revealed their easy home life. Newspapers had grown to an enormous mountain beside a faded chintz chair, and there were some glasses abandoned on the coffee table.

"You can wait here," she said, turning to Abel. "Or get a drink from the kitchen, if you like. It's through that door. If you meet someone back there, it's my roommate. Her name's Carly Moffat."

"Won't she be startled if a strange man walks into her kitchen?"

"Despite what you think, you're not the first man I've brought home without warning. Besides, she's probably out in the garden. She's planting herbs."

"Where are you going?"

"Upstairs to change. I'll only be a moment. Help yourself to a drink."

Abel wanted to follow her, but he held himself back. He could hear Samantha start to hum as she trotted up the stairs, and he wondered why she sounded so pleased with herself all of a sudden. He grinned. What did she have up her sleeve? He couldn't resist a peek at her legs as she disappeared up the stairway. Fabulous.

When he heard a door close quietly upstairs, he took a quick tour of her house. He soon discovered that Samantha and her roommate listened to vintage show tunes, read an enormous variety of magazines, and bought gourmet popcorn in huge tin barrels.

Their state-of-the-art kitchen revealed that one of the women was an expert cook. Expensive pots hung from a suspended rack, assorted gadgets lined the counters, and an impressive array of knives stuck out of a fat, wooden block.

Sitting on the counter was the picnic basket he'd sent that morning. Abel grinned. It was open, and the contents had been rifled. Bits of packing straw were scattered on the counter. Beside the basket was the note Abel had written to Samantha. Someone had crumpled the note into a ball, then carefully flattened it out again to read a second time. Abel found himself very pleased about that. He was making progress.

He heard someone scraping with a shovel beyond the back door and peeked through lace curtains to see a trim young woman digging in her garden with fierce concentration. Better not disturb her, he thought. He found a beer in the refrigerator and was drinking from the bottle when Samantha reappeared, a transformed woman.

Abel nearly choked on his beer. Gone was the cool professional. She had changed her suit for a pair of sleek black spandex leggings that clung to every curve of her beautiful backside and those long, delicious thighs. She looked incredible—and ten years younger than she did in the prim executive clothes she usually wore.

Over leggings, she had on a snug white T-shirt, but as she arrived, she pulled a bulky, long-sleeved shirt over it. Abel caught the outline of her small breasts and the nip of her narrow waist. He barely controlled his urge to drop the beer and slip his hands around her hips to measure their firmness. Samantha Wyatt was in tip-top physical shape.

"You've made yourself at home, I see," she said. "Did you meet Carly?"

"Not yet," Abel said, his voice ridiculously hoarse.

She perched on a kitchen stool and pulled on her running shoes. She had drawn her black hair into a jaunty ponytail that curled temptingly around her ear and brushed her shoulder as she talked.

"Carly's been my roommate for a couple of years," she said, unaware of the uproar she was causing in his brain. "We get along well because she doesn't work for the government. I can come home and put my work out of my mind if I want to."

Abel had a grip on himself by then. "What does she do?"

"She's the assistant food editor of the *Post*."

With his beer, he gestured at the pots overhead. "That explains the hardware."

"They're certainly not mine. Carly's a real expert. She cooks wonderful meals, and I do the dishes. I'm afraid my talents weren't meant for the kitchen."

"Some women use their talents in other rooms," Abel said—just to needle her. "Personally, I like to cook. When I lived in Paris, I got hooked on open-air produce markets that—"

"You lived in Paris?" Samantha looked at him in surprise, shoelaces suspended in her fingers.

"Yeah." It was time to dazzle her with the better parts of his checkered past. "I went to school there for a while. And I go back occasionally."

"To visit? Or work?"

"Both. I have a lot of friends in France."

Studying his face as if to guess what other secrets he could be hiding, Samantha said, "We haven't talked much about you."

"Until now, you haven't given me a chance."

"After we run," Samantha said firmly, "I want a complete history." She finished tying her shoe and stood up.

Abel nearly took her in his arms then. She was beautiful and a little cocky now—no longer afraid. He had to restrain himself with an effort. Going running with her didn't sound nearly as appealing as curling up on the nearest sofa for a long heart-to-heart and some heavy petting.

Longingly he asked, "Why don't we skip the run and talk now?"

"Because," she said deliberately, "I'd rather have you exhausted before we're alone together. You'll be easier to handle. Shall we stretch outside?"

He grinned. "Lead the way."

Abel followed her back through the living room and out the front door. On the steps, he did his best to mimic Samantha as she went through a series of contortions calculated to stretch every muscle in the human body. Quickly Abel realized that Miss Samantha Wyatt knew exactly what she was doing. He always stretched a little before playing racquetball, but nothing like the complicated exercises Samantha put him through. When she pronounced herself ready, she led the way out onto the sidewalk and set off down the street at a brisk clip.

Within six blocks, Abel knew he was in *big* trouble. His shirt was starting to stick to his chest, and his breath wasn't coming as smoothly as he thought it would.

"Is this pace all right for you?" Samantha asked when they paused at an intersection to wait for the traffic to pass. She ran in place, her feet hardly tapping the sidewalk, her bright hair bouncing in its ponytail. Her face sparkled with the pleasure of being out in the fresh air. Her tight body gleamed in its spandex suit.

"It's great," Abel said, trying to smile instead of pant. "When are we really going to cut loose?"

"Right now," she said. "Let's go!"

She led him down the street, along the sidewalks, across a bridge, beneath an underpass, across a courtyard, along the canal tow path, through a tunnel, up a hill, down a hill. She ran and ran and ran and showed no signs whatsoever of tiring. It was a complete tour of Georgetown, and if Abel had been capable of concentrating on anything but his own cardiovascular system, he might have enjoyed the trip. Watching Samantha's perfect body would have been a joy. As it was, after a few miles Abel began to worry he might have to stop and throw up. His shirt was soaked with sweat and even his socks were starting to feel soggy.

Samantha ran lightly along the sidewalks, calling encouragement to him now and then, but mostly looking wonderfully vital and lovely as she flew along. Her ponytail danced, her legs flashed, her laughter seemed to caress the air.

"Tell me when you'd like to slow down," she gaily called to him over her shoulder. "I can go forever!"

"I'm fine," Abel croaked, stumbling to keep up with her as evening began to gather around them. Frantically he tried to come up with a way to cheat—a way to beat her at her own game.

But suddenly he caught his foot on a crack in the sidewalk and nearly sprawled flat on his face. Samantha glanced over her shoulder just in time to see him grab a tree for dear life.

She circled back to him, still running effortlessly, and he hung to the tree trunk for support. "Are you okay?"

"Of course!"

She was smiling. "Had enough, Abel?"

"Only—only if you have," he gasped.

"I'm a little winded," she said, and he would have kissed her if he'd had the energy. "Let's head for home," she added.

Did he dare trip her? Knock her to the ground?

You couldn't knock over a dachshund, he told himself.

Thank heaven they were only a block from her place. He barely made it through the gate and into a small courtyard behind her house. He collapsed on the porch steps, no longer caring what Samantha thought. He puffed like an overheated locomotive and dimly heard her call, "Carly! Bring a glass of water! I've got a dying man out here!"

In a moment she was pressing a glass into his hands and guiding it to his lips. "Take a sip, Abel. It might help."

"I'm okay," he panted. "Really. Oh, hello."

Obviously amused by his attempt to appear normal, a small, blond woman folded her arms across her chest. "There's one lesson I learned the first week I moved in here, and that's not to try keeping up with Samantha. She used to run marathons, you know."

"She just did," Abel gasped. "Or maybe two."

Samantha patted his back. "We didn't go that far," she assured him. "But it might have been five or six miles. You should have *said* something. Carly, this is Abel Fletcher. Abel, meet my roommate, Carly Moffat."

Abel waved weakly. "Forgive me for not getting up."

Carly and Samantha exchanged grins, then Carly zipped up the porch steps. "You need some orange juice, I think, to get your electrolytes back in balance. Hang on, Abel. I know exactly how to treat exhaustion. Samantha's brought back guys in worse shape than you are."

"Did they live?" Abel bleated.

"Most of 'em," Carly replied, and then she disappeared inside.

Samantha sat on the step beside him. "Honestly, Abel, I didn't realize you were so tired."

"I'm not," he said, risking a sip of water. He choked, then swallowed hard. "I just—I guess that last hill got me."

"You did very well up until then," Samantha assured him, patting his heaving shoulder. "Really, you were terrific."

He groaned. "Stop! It sounds like you're talking about impotency."

Samantha laughed and the sound caused Abel to start feeling better.

Carly returned at that moment. She handed glasses of juice and a hand towel to each of them before winking at Samantha and disappearing once more. Samantha used her towel to dry the sheen of perspiration from her face, then she turned her attention to Abel and proceeded to do the same for him. He sat still while she wiped the worst of the sweat from his brow.

"Take a little sip," she cautioned. "Not too much or you'll be sick."

Abel drank some juice, and in a few minutes he began to feel increasingly healthy. He noticed that Samantha still looked annoyingly fresh. Her face glowed and the muscles in her legs shimmered under tights. She looked magnificent. Abel asked, "How often do you run like that?"

She smiled, still daubing him with the towel. "Two or three times a week, depending on the weather. I'm out of shape. I used to do it every day."

Abel sighed, then took the towel from Samantha's hand and finished drying his face and throat. He decided to be honest. "I'm too old for this."

"Nonsense."

"No, I've been told by a friend that I'm getting old. Maybe I ought to believe him."

"I doubt you'll ever be old. It's a state of mind, you know."

She was smiling at him. "You're something, lady," he said, shaking his head in admiration. "I'm impressed as hell. Not only can you run like a gazelle, but you manage to look fantastic afterward."

Samantha watched him for a minute, and her smile began to grow. There was an odd look in her eyes also. She was re-evaluating, Abel could see. Weighing the chances. The cool poker player was sizing up the possibilities.

Her face was cast in shadow, but a sliver of light from the kitchen caught her eyes. They were surprisingly warm, as she gazed steadily back at him, and filled with flickers of light that weren't the result of exercise. Abel began to wonder what she was thinking, and his pulse began to thump all over again. They were very much alone together, and Samantha's expression was suddenly alive with speculation.

She said, "A lesser man would have given up, you know."

"I hate to give up on anything."

"Especially when your pride is at stake."

She laughed, and her smile was enough to make Abel catch his breath. When he could speak, he said, "If I had an ounce of energy, I'd consider trying to kiss you right now."

Softly she said, "*You* might be exhausted, but I've still got a little energy left."

With that she leaned forward and kissed him— lightly—on the mouth. She surprised the hell out of him. Unconsciously Abel lifted his hand to touch her cheek, to hold her there an instant longer, to savor the moment. His heart suddenly accelerated out of control. She didn't draw back but parted her lips ever so slightly and licked his tongue with hers. Abel's brain went blank with desire. Then it was over, and she was once more sitting back and looking at him with her green eyes full of mystery.

Breathless all over again, he said in a husky murmur, "What was that for?"

"I'm not sure. Curiosity maybe. Or reward for being a good sport."

He allowed a grin. "I was a better sport than that, Samantha. I was a *damn* good sport, don't you think?"

He grabbed her head and pulled her close for another kiss, longer this time, and he flicked his tongue along the outer contour of her mouth. She murmured something against his lips, but Abel was too lost in the flood of sensations to hear properly. She tasted sweet and salty and hot, and when he leaned into the kiss and pressed her mouth farther open, Samantha let him take charge. He kissed her long and thoroughly after that. It was delicious. Arousing. And not just for him. When he finally lessened the contact until their lips were barely clinging to each other, Samantha gave a soft shiver of excitement.

When she opened her brilliant green eyes, he said quietly, "Maybe if I was an *exceptionally* good sport, we could move this party to more comfortable quarters."

Samantha laughed, her whole expression sparkling with recklessness. "Right now, you couldn't walk if you tried!"

"You'll get to know me better," he promised, leaning back on his elbow and letting his long legs stretch out alongside Samantha's shapely ones. He drank some juice. "You'll find I recover very quickly in spite of my age."

She liked the fact that he hadn't pushed for more kisses. Impulsively she said, "I would like to know you better. At times you don't seem like such a—"

"A thug?"

"Something like that. The Speaker obviously learned a thing or two about you that made him trust you."

"What do you want to know?"

"The works. Where you come from, who your friends are—"

What did he have to lose? Abel told her. They relaxed on the steps and drank juice and cooled off while he talked. He told her about his family in Montana, school in the Ivy League, later study at the Sorbonne. He talked about the fluke that got him started at the museum, and chose to modestly gloss over most of his adventures in acquiring extraordinary exhibits. There would be time for bragging later. Then, in a burst of uncharacteristic candor, he even mentioned Elizabeth.

"Were you in love with her?" Samantha asked when he was finished.

"Yes," he said. And surprising even himself, he added, "But not enough, I guess. She hated competing with my work, and in the end, the work won."

"You didn't marry her."

"Nope. She wanted a family, a dog, and a station wagon, and she knew I wasn't going to settle down to life in suburbia."

Samantha digested that. Abel couldn't guess what she was thinking. She had controlled her face again and avoided meeting his gaze. That was her trick, he realized. She knew her eyes gave her inner thoughts away.

But suddenly she said, "Stay for dinner."

He laughed. "What? A change of heart?"

"Not completely," she said. "I still think you're peculiar."

"But my magnetic charm is working wonders on you."

Her smile was wry. "Maybe. Anyway, you can stay a little longer. Carly's cooking something exquisite, I'm sure, and you can have a shower, if you like. We can probably dig up something for you to wear.''

"I've got some clean clothes in my car.''

She raised one delicate eyebrow. "You came prepared, didn't you?''

"Completely,'' he replied, spirits rising.

Five

Playing with fire. That's what Samantha figured she was doing. She heard Abel singing a medley of Buddy Holly hits in the shower and wondered if she'd lost her mind.

She showered in the other bathroom, then pulled on a cotton jumpsuit and hurried to the kitchen where Carly was entertaining Abel. He was cleaned up and dressed again, and met Samantha with a matter-of-fact kiss on the mouth, one that sent tingles to the tips of all her nerve endings. He was holding Peaches in his capable arms, and the cat purred with delight.

"You got dressed too fast," he said to Samantha, releasing the cat. "Your buttons are crooked."

Samantha stood still while he took his time fixing the situation. She held her breath, quaking inside as his long fingers lingered over the task, and watching his expression—which was far from angelic. He finished rearranging the buttons of her jumpsuit and passed a slight caress down the curve of her cheek.

"There," he said. "Perfect again."

"Abel and I have been getting acquainted," Carly said. "He's feeling better. Abel, would you mind going down to the cellar for a bottle of wine to go with our dinner?"

"Is this a ruse to get rid of me?"

"So we can talk about you, yes. Be a good boy and run along."

When the two women were alone again, Carly said, "He's definitely unusual, Sam. A little rough around the edges for you, I think."

"He's a menace," Samantha retorted, lifting fluted glasses from their rack. The glassware rattled together, revealing how her hands were still trembling.

"He looks at you like you're the best thing since whipped cream."

Weakly Samantha said, "I know."

"This is a very dangerous situation," Carly teased, wagging her head. "He's a real rogue, Samantha. Not to mention an intelligent man in the body of a god. I think you're in trouble."

"You don't know the half of it!"

"Anything I can do to help?"

"Just stay on your guard. I assume he's going to try to charm you so I'll think he's harmless."

"He's anything but harmless," Carly retorted. "You lucky girl."

Carly's menu for the evening included a clear soup, tender slices of duck cooked very fast with cucumbers and four cloves of garlic, steamed vegetables in a tart dressing, plus a fancy cake topped with meringue and hazelnuts. What made the meal memorable was not the food, however, but the camaraderie which gradually evolved while the three of them prepared the courses. Sipping wine and talking with a great deal of laughter, they shared the cooking chores and kitchen anecdotes. Abel stirred vegetables and revealed that he'd once blown up his mother's kitchen experimenting with a pressure cooker, while Carly wielded her tasting spoon and described the day she squirted decorating frosting all over a five-star chef.

Getting cautiously into the spirit of things, Samantha admitted that she made the best chocolate chip cookies east of the Rockies.

"So you have a domestic side, after all?" Abel noted.

"Don't let her kid you," Carly spoke up. "Samantha would rather argue legislations with a roomful of Harvard lawyers than boil an egg."

"I know my priorities," Samantha said. "And I like chocolate chip cookies more than boiled eggs."

When the food was ready, they helped themselves out of the pots and ate around the cooking island, elbows on the counter, feet hooked on the rungs of their stools.

Samantha kept a watchful eye on Abel throughout the evening. He had put on a blue polo shirt and jeans—nothing elegant, but clothes that emphasized that he was every inch a man. A virile, exciting man who had earned the right to be cocky, she suspected. She could see he'd been around the world, and the adventures he'd spoken so offhandedly about earlier hadn't been as casual as he'd let on. He'd found himself in a danger and escaped by using his wits.

His hair was wet and slicked back in such a way that it drew Samantha's attention to the shape of his nose, which had obviously been broken once. That set her to thinking, too. No doubt he was lethal in a fistfight. But he was also capable of washing dishes without being asked and did so—if a little awkwardly, which showed he wasn't completely domesticated.

On top of all that, he could also make her laugh.

"Did you know," he said when he was elbow-deep in soap suds, "that it's possible to create nuclear fusion at room temperature using gin and vermouth? It happened in my hotel room in Mexico City once."

"Hold it, everybody," Carly called. She was waving her Polaroid camera. "We can't cut the cake until I take a photo."

"Of us?" Abel grabbed Samantha around the waist and struck a movie poster pose. He loomed over her arched body like Cary Grant demanding a kiss from his leading lady. "How's this?"

Carly laughed. "No, you idiot. I want a picture of the cake!"

Abel's grip slackened and he looked bewildered.

"Carly keeps a file," Samantha explained, extricating herself from his embrace. "She clips her recipes to pictures of the final product. It's part of her job."

Carly began clicking away, but she didn't limit herself to photos of her creation this time. Samantha noticed she managed to get a number of shots of Abel and Samantha. Then Abel took the camera away from Carly and staged some shots of her posing with the cake, cutting the cake, eating the cake—and spitting out a mouthful when she realized she'd goofed on the recipe. In time, they were laughing again. Samantha surreptitiously slipped one of the photos of Abel into her pocket.

After the dishes were dried and put away, Carly shooed them out of the kitchen. "I have to make some notes on the food," she said. "So leave me alone."

Abel checked his watch. "I should be leaving, anyway. Thanks, Carly. You've been great."

He kissed her on the cheek, and Carly—usually a cool cookie—turned three shades of red and pushed him out the door. Instinctively Abel took hold of Samantha's hand as she led him out of the brightly lit kitchen and into the quiet darkness of the living room.

Alone with him, Samantha said. "You managed to sweep my roommate off her feet."

He needed no more encouragement than that to halt in his tracks and sweep Samantha into his arms again. His grin was infuriatingly self-assured. And bone-tinglingly sexy. "How am I doing with you?"

She braced her hands on his chest, noticing there was no stopping him when he wanted to hold her. She was breathless and tried to hide it. "I'll withhold judgment a little longer."

"How about some dessert while you make up your mind?" He dipped close and nuzzled his nose through her hair. His breath tickled her earlobe. "Would you like to finish the evening with something sweet and delicious?"

"There's an ice-cream shop four blocks from here, if that's what you mean."

"I can't walk that far," he replied, laughing under his breath. "Not after what you put me through."

"You don't seem to be suffering."

He molded her body to fit against his more intimately. He felt good—so very good that Samantha bid farewell to the last of her crumbling willpower. She released a sigh, and he smiled.

Holding her in the powerful curve of his left arm, he used his right had to tug the clip that held her hair in its ponytail. He dropped the clip to the floor and forgot it. Gently combing his fingers through the loosened strands, he spoke in that same low, intimate voice he'd used before. "You're not afraid of me anymore, are you?"

Samantha's laugh quivered. "Oh, I'm afraid, all right!"

He straightened and looked into her eyes, probing for the truth. "Are you?"

"Not that you're going to murder me," she corrected, unable to quell the trembling inside herself. She slid her hands to his muscled arms to keep her balance. "But—"

"I would never hurt you."

"Not physically," Samantha said cautiously, risking a glance up into his dark gaze.

"Aha," said Abel, and he came closer to brush tiny kisses down her cheekbone.

"Abel—" she began.

"I love to hear you say my name." His voice was husky with unsuppressed desire. He kissed her mouth long and deliciously before sliding his lips down her jawline to the place where her pulse beat like frantic butterfly wings. Samantha could sense him smiling.

And she was melting. Inside, hot liquid sensations had begun to warm her most womanly places. Samantha tilted her head back to allow him full access to the sensitive flesh of her throat. She clung to Abel's strong frame, conscious of how their bodies fit together as though they'd been welded.

Samantha cleared her throat. "I'm a good girl, you know. No one-night stands, no quickie relationships."

He hooked his forefinger under her chin and forced her to look up at him. His smile was wicked. "You want a good conduct medal?"

Samantha couldn't smile back. "I've got my job to think about."

He stroked her chin as if she were a purring cat. "What does that have to do with me?"

"Listen to what I have to say, all right?" Screwing up her courage, she said, "Usually when someone comes on strong to me, I get suspicious."

"Of what?" He was attentive suddenly, frowning as he studied her expression.

"I've got a position of power," Samantha continued steadily. "I'm often approached to do favors for people. I am wooed by many men, and when one of them gets as familiar as you're getting, I assume he's got a political agenda on his mind."

"Politics," muttered Abel, gathering her breathlessly close. "That's the last thing on my mind right now. Are you wearing a bra? It's been driving me crazy all night."

"Abel, listen to me!" Samantha fought to keep him from bending her body to his will. "I mean it. I have to know you're not manipulating me for your own reasons."

"My reasons are purely romantic."

"I did some research today. There's a bill coming up in Congress—museum funding. We're expecting pressure from the Smithsonian."

Abel's face turned hard suddenly as he looked down at her. "You think I've got something to do with that?"

"It's logical. In fact, it happens to me all the time. I almost expect it when I meet someone for the first—"

"Don't talk like that!" Abel gripped her fiercely. "I have nothing to do with funding. Hell, if you knew the kinds of things I do in my job, you'd see I'm the last man they'd choose for bureaucratic slap and tickle."

"All right," she said, humoring him. "Whatever you say. But don't expect me to—"

"You don't trust me at all, do you?"

"Not really."

"I was a perfect gentleman tonight! It was damned hard, but I did it."

"Maybe you were too perfect."

"Dammit, Samantha!"

"Don't expect me to throw myself into your arms without a second thought," she said, trying to stay calm. "I'm not stupid."

"And I'm not patient," he snapped. "Not where you're concerned."

"Then we might as well say goodbye tonight."

"I can't do that, Samantha."

"I can."

"No, you can't. I can see what's really going on in your pretty head, Samantha. I think you'd like to stop talking right now and get on with something much more entertaining."

She looked away, intending to keep the rest of her thoughts as secret as possible. "Abel—"

His mouth found hers, crushing her lips, seeking her tongue with his own and plundering the inside of her mouth as if searching for treasure. He laced his fingers through her hair, using that leverage to hold her lips fast to his, then moving his mouth over hers in a quick, tantalizing sexual rhythm. Samantha heard a moan of pleasure—and realized it was her own. Without thinking, she smoothed her hands up his tense shoulders until her arms found their way around his neck. She held him tightly, pressing against his rock-hard frame.

Abel uttered her name hoarsely—as if tortured by desire. He caressed her neck and suddenly cupped her breast through the fabric of her jumpsuit. He discovered she'd worn no bra as her nipple blossomed against his palm. Samantha felt her body respond to his touch all the way down to the hollow between her thighs, and she shuddered at the intensity.

"You like that, don't you?" he whispered, caressing her breast.

"Yes."

"And this?" He began to unfasten the buttons of the jumpsuit, still kissing her lips, her cheeks, her temples. Samantha didn't stop him. She couldn't summon the strength. When he'd managed to undo half of them, he slid his warm hand inside and cupped her bare flesh.

"That, too," she murmured, trying to catch her breath. "But it doesn't mean—"

"Wait," he said.

Abruptly he tugged at two more buttons and then pulled the jumpsuit off her shoulders. He eased it down, baring her breasts to the moonlight that pierced the curtains. His hungry gaze seemed to brand her naked skin. His eyes devoured her—and caused an erotic wave that flowed through Samantha's limbs, suffusing her with excitement. Slowly he began more caresses, sliding his fingertips around and around her nipples until they ached. He watched her eyes as if mesmerized.

"I love seeing you aroused like this," he said. "Your eyes are beautiful, and your mouth—"

He kissed her mouth to make his point, then groaned with pleasure when Samantha met his tongue with her own coaxing, teasing motions. She couldn't stop herself. His need for her was intoxicating. She'd never known a man who wanted her so badly. It was a heady feeling to be so desirable, so hungered for. It was enough to drive a woman beyond reason.

She tried to shake her head. "Wait. We should stop."

"Why?" he murmured. "We're both attracted to each other."

"Sexual attraction isn't enough for me. Abel, we're two completely different kinds of people!"

"Haven't you heard? Opposites attract!"

"But not for long. If you want quick, fun sex, why don't you go find someone who—"

"I don't want someone else. I want you!"

"*Why?* Why me, Abel? Of all the women in Washington, why have you chosen me?"

He fought with himself for a second, clearly wrestling with a choice. "If I tell you, you won't believe me."

She slipped her jumpsuit back in place. "Of course I will."

"It's—it's—oh, hell, Samantha! Can't we just enjoy what fate has done for us?"

"Fate? No, no, I can't do that. Not until I'm sure I can trust you."

"I'm telling you, I have nothing to do with any funding bill!" He gripped her shoulders. "If someone got the brilliant idea of seducing you, don't you think they'd pick a better lover than me?"

Samantha had to laugh. "You're not so bad," she said, smiling.

That startled him and he began to grin a little. "No kidding?"

"Well, I'm not a terribly good judge. There have been other men in my life, but—"

"Shut up."

He kissed her to prevent more discussion on that subject. When his lips finally left hers a languorous minute later, he murmured, "I don't want to hear about other men. Never again, understand?" With a powerful undercurrent in his voice he said, "I'm your only man now, Samantha. Don't forget it." Another kiss almost drained her dry of any common sense.

But Abel left after that, saying nothing more. Samantha stood at the open door and watched him stride into the darkness, unsteadily hanging onto the doorknob for support. She wasn't sure she could stand alone. Warmed to her very core, she watched him go and finally closed the door.

Dreamily she pulled the photo from her pocket and studied it. Abel's grin shone back at her—complete with the look of wicked amusement that turned her bones to jelly. Looking at the photo, Samantha began to smile.

Abel hustled into the museum half an hour later. He knew he wasn't going to be able to sleep, so he let himself into the office section of the Smithsonian and made his way down the stairs to his own room.

The Smithsonian was affectionately known as the "Nation's Attic," and the name served it well. The many buildings were full of collections so vast and varied that it was the ultimate pack rat's paradise. Normally Abel reveled in its celebration of man's endeavors, but not this night.

Now he could only think of one thing.

Arriving in the basement, he noticed a light under one of the office doors and burst into the office without knocking.

Oliver jumped a foot and cried out. "Man! Have a heart, will you?"

"I *do* have a heart," Abel growled, "that's my problem."

"Where have you been?" Oliver asked, pushing aside the microscope on his desk. "I hope you've been at home working on your report. The boss is starting to think you've run back to Kimi Lau. Where *have* you been?"

"Making love to a woman, dammit!"

Oliver grinned. "That's odd. Usually a guy sounds happy when he says something like that."

"I *am* happy. At least I think I am." Abel cursed, raking his fingers through his hair. "I don't know what's happening to me. All I can think about is her!"

"Great! Who is she? What's she like?"

"She's warm and sexy and beautiful and—and oh, damn, she's the most spectacular female that's ever come into my life." Abel plunked down onto one of Oliver's stools and buried his face in his hands—miserable and exhausted and tense enough to snap like a too-tightened violin string.

"Wow," Oliver breathed. "How the mighty have fallen."

Abel pulled himself together and glared at his colleague. "Don't repeat a word of this, Oliver, or I'll break your neck, but last night I found myself wandering all over the city, and guess where I finally ended up?"

"Where?"

"Staring at the display window at Babyland! Is that something a sane man would do?"

Oliver smothered a laugh. "N—no,l I don't think so."

"Of course it's not! And it's all the fault of this damned stone!"

He grabbed the Kimi Lauan charm out of his pocket and threw it on Oliver's desk.

"The stone?" Oliver said blankly.

"Yes, it's made me crazy!"

"Let me get this straight. You think this stone has something to do with this woman you've been seeing?"

"Yes! It's—it's—oh, hell, I think the damn thing has made me fall in love with her!"

Oliver stared. "Are you kidding?"

"Do I *look* like I'm kidding?"

"Have you told her yet?"

"About the stone? Hell, no. Would you believe a story like this, if you were her?"

"I don't believe it, and I'm not even one of the principal players. Abel, are you serious? A drunken island chief gives you a cheap souvenir, and you think it's got magic power?"

"What else can it be? I would never act like this unless something supernatural had intervened. All I know is that unless I'm with her, I feel like I'm going to die."

"Maybe you're just in love with her in the normal way."

"The *normal* way? You think normal guys feel this way? How can we expect to continue the species if we're all crazy?"

Oliver shrugged. "I've seen some pretty ordinary guys go nuts when the right woman comes along."

"Well, right now I'm more nuts than any man on the face of the earth." Abel got up and began to pace. "It's this charm, I'm sure. Maybe we'd better do something, Oliver."

"We?" he repeated uncertainly.

"Yes, we could reverse the spell—make it go away or something."

"Would that make any difference?"

Abel stopped pacing. "What?"

"I mean, if we found a way to end the magic, would you really want to do it? Wouldn't you still be crazy about this lady?"

Abel frowned. The kid was right. He couldn't imagine a life without Samantha. Not anymore. She was the center of his universe now, the most beautiful element in his life.

Abel grabbed the stone and glared at it, wishing he'd never laid eyes on the evil thing. But the painted figures seemed to laugh back at him, dancing across the river-smoothed surface of rock. He was bewitched. He closed his eyes and groaned.

"Look," said Oliver, "Why don't you just admit that you love her, ask if she'll marry you, then settle down and start making babies? Your troubles will be over!"

Abel sat down again. "Maybe they'd just be starting. What if the magic wears off?"

"Do you think it will?"

"It might. I have no control over it, Oliver. I'm telling you, I'm completely at the mercy of this thing! What if I wake up someday and find myself chained to a woman I hardly know? What then?"

Oliver sighed. "Abel, I think you're going through what every man goes through at your stage in life. You're in love, but it scares the hell out of you."

"You got that right," Abel sighed.

Six

The morning after her dinner with Abel, Samantha wasn't feeling much like concentrating on her work. Then her well-organized schedule for Tuesday was blown to smithereens when a crisis came up in the Speaker's home district. Rains in the northern part of the state caused flooding and ruined a great many fields owned by farmers who telephoned the office asking for federal help. To get her mind off Abel Fletcher, Samantha assigned herself the job of taking care of their needs to make sure things were handled quickly and precisely.

By the end of the day, the farmers had been taken care of, and she had completely forgotten about Abel.

Or so she thought.

"You okay, Samantha?" Speaker Glendenning called when she marched past his open office door.

Samantha backed up a pace. "Certainly. Why do you ask?"

"Well, honey," he said, looking at her with his bushy brows raised in amusement, "I wasn't aware of that new style you've got on."

"What new style?"

"Wearing your coat inside out. That is a new style, isn't it? You're not letting your mind wander, are you?"

Hastily Samantha peeled off her coat, turned it right side out, and put it back on again. "It was a simple mistake," she said defensively to her chortling boss. "Anyone could do it."

"Sure, sure," said the Speaker, and he laughed uproariously."

Samantha left the office in a hurry before she made an even bigger fool of herself. When she started down the stone steps in front of the building, though, she saw Abel Fletcher leaning against the hood of an illegally parked car.

A few Capitol employees were leaving the office building and eyed Fletcher warily as they passed. He was wearing his leather flight jacket again and looked like he'd just escaped from the nearest stalag. Passersby gave him a wide berth.

"Samantha!"

He came up the steps with the grace of a starving carnivore.

"Come on," he said, taking her elbow in a way that permitted no argument.

"What are you doing?" Alarmed, Samantha resisted his grip.

"Kidnapping you." Effortlessly he pulled her down the steps. "In an hour you can decide if you like it or not. I hear it's a popular fantasy among certain kinds of women.''

"What do you know about women's fantasies?"

"Enough to know when to take advantage of them." He popped open the passenger door of the car and looked down at Samantha's face with a grin. "What's your favorite fantasy?"

"You mean like winning the lottery?"

His grin broadened. "No, I mean what you dream about in your bed at night before you fall asleep."

"Are we talking about lately?" she asked archly. "Or before you showed up?"

He tipped her chin up until their gazes met. In a husky voice, he asked, "Do you dream about being carried off by a man who considers you his magnificent obsession?"

"Is that what you're doing? Carrying me off?"

"Are you afraid?"

"Should I be?"

"Come on, Samantha. You've played it safe all your life. Take a chance for once."

She laughed. "All right, you may have an hour of my time, Mr. Fletcher."

"Done." He pulled the passenger door wide and drew the handle of Samantha's briefcase from her hand. "Will you join me, please?"

"Good heavens. I believe that's the first time I've heard you use that word."

"Please? It was a momentary lapse. It'll pass, I'm sure. Get in."

"Yes, sir."

Samantha got into his car. It was an old Swedish compact with a cracked dashboard and a torn seat, but otherwise it was clean inside and out. She was a little surprised to discover that Abel took care of his property. He didn't seem the type.

When Abel got in beside her and started the car, the engine turned over at once and purred like a pampered kitten—another surprise.

"Where are we going?" she asked when he pulled out onto the street.

"To my lair," he replied.

He drove a short distance down the Mall, turned and started back, then whipped the car into an alley between the huge museums. A parking spot marked with his name lay halfway along the alley.

"If you have your own parking space," Samantha said lightly, "you could have just about any woman in Washington."

"I don't want just any woman," he said, and got out of the car.

He didn't bother locking it and came around the hood in time to help Samantha out. "This way," he said, pulling her to a side entrance of the museum where he used his own key to gain entry.

"Abel, it's after hours. Are we allowed to do this?"

"They hate it when I use this door at night—I'm supposed to check in at the desk. But that's a waste of time. Ah—here we go."

Protesting, Samantha was dragged into the museum and down a flight of stairs. Abel ignored her pleas to follow the rules and strode quickly along the darkened corridors. Samantha hustled to keep up with his long strides.

"Will you give me a clue," she panted, "about what we're doing here?"

"I'm taking you to the inner sanctum," he replied over is shoulder. "To prove how trustworthy I am. Or not, as the case may be. Good—he hasn't left yet."

They arrived in a carpeted reception area that was manned by a single late-staying secretary who looked up from her typewriter and immediately panicked.

"Dr. Fletcher! What do you think you're doing?"

"Doctor?" Samantha asked.

"Don't mind us, Sylvie," Able called, not breaking stride but heading for a firmly closed office door. "We're just going to have a word with the big guy."

"But he's not to be disturbed! He gave strict orders—"

Abel barged through the door anyway, hauling Samantha behind him. "Henry," he said, "I need your help."

The proper little man sitting behind the huge mahogany desk jerked in surprise, and the tediously assembled skeleton he was intently studying quivered in his hands and shattered into a hundred pieces.

"Fletcher!" he shrieked. "Now look what you've done!"

"What? Another cat skeleton for your collection, Henry? When are you going to give up that gruesome hobby?"

The balding man behind the desk leaped to his feet, trembling with rage as he pointed at the heap of splintered bones. "It is not just another skeleton, Fletcher, it was my mother's cat Clementine! I promised I'd have those bones ready for Mother's Day!"

"Your mother must be as unbalanced as you are, Henry."

"*Unbalanced*? Who's talking about unbalanced? Fletcher, I should fire you on this very spot! If I threw you out this minute I—I—well, for one thing I'd never see that report of yours. Where is it, may I ask? How do you expect this museum to run efficiently if you—"

"You'll get your report as soon as I can blackmail somebody into writing it for me. Now shut up a minute and listen—this is important. I want you to meet someone. This is Samantha Wyatt. She works for Speaker Glendenning. Samantha, this is Henry Boswell."

"Hello," Samantha said, trying to catch her breath and shake Mr. Boswell's hand at the same time.

Boswell looked mystified and uneasily straightened his tie. "How do you do, Miss Wyatt? What's going on here?

"I wish I knew," she replied.

"Sit down, everybody," Fletcher commanded, pulling up a chair for Samantha and then collapsing into another for himself. He propped his boots on the edge of Henry Boswell's desk and made himself at home.

"Now then," he began cheerfully. "Henry, Miss Wyatt is under the impression that I have something to do with asking congress for more money for the museum. She thinks I've been sent to infiltrate the Speaker's office to help our cause."

"Our cause?" Boswell repeated, sinking back into his own chair. "Since when do you concern yourself with museum politics?"

"Exactly," Abel said with satisfaction. "Now tell her I have nothing to do with that kind of stuff."

"Fletcher, who in their right mind—excuse me, Miss Wyatt—would ever imagine you worry about where our money comes from? All you do is spend it like there's no tomorrow!"

Abel looked affronted. "I do not! I'm very careful about money, Henry. I take a tent wherever I go, don't I? You don't get big hotel bills from me, or first-class plane fare, or—"

"What about that episode with the Turkish masseuse?"

"That was a mistake," Abel conceded at once. "I gave her the wrong credit card. I fixed that with Accounting. I spend the money where it counts—on getting exhibits back here in the best possible shape. Come on, Henry, help me!"

Boswell glared at his troublemaking employee. "After all the pain you've caused me, Fletcher, why do you think I might be the slightest bit interested in helping you?"

"Because secretly you admire my work?"

Boswell sighed like a man holding onto his patience by the merest thread and transferred his gaze to Samantha. "Miss Wyatt," he said slowly, "I can't imagine why an obviously intelligent woman like you is interested in this man's activities, but I can assure you that Fletcher is in no way involved in any museum business except those duties he performs as only he can. He's our expert in vintage aircraft and spends most of his time in the field or conducting research at our restoration facility. Otherwise, he's absolutely useless."

"See?" Abel asked Samantha triumphantly. "They think I'm useless!"

"In fact," Boswell continued, warming to his subject, "Fletcher is the biggest pain in the neck I've ever encountered. He's unreliable, uncommunicative—"

"She gets the point," Abel said.

"Reckless, foolhardy—"

"Okay, *okay*!"

"In short," said Boswell sternly, "I don't allow him to participate in anything that might jeopardize the actual operation of our museum. He is the proverbial bull in the china closet."

"So I've noticed," Samantha said at last.

"Has he been annoying you, Miss Wyatt?" Boswell asked hopefully. "If you registered a complaint, perhaps we could have him arrested! Maybe in jail he'd finish the report I need."

"I don't think we need to call the police just yet," Samantha said with a smile. "Mr. Boswell, I wonder if you have any written material that concerns the museum funding bill that's coming up before Congress soon? I'd be happy to take your position paper back to my office."

Boswell brightened. "How nice of you! Yes, I have a copy of our opinions on the funding bill. It's here somewhere. Let me ask Sylvie. She's the one who really runs things around here."

Boswell hurried out of the office, leaving Samantha and Abel alone. Abel took his boots off the desk and stood up, looking sulky. "Why did you ask for a position paper?"

"I'd like to read up on the subject," Samantha replied, rising to her feet also.

"When?"

"No time like the present. Tonight of course."

"That's what I was afraid of. I was hoping we could have dinner at my place."

She laughed. "Were you planning to cook for me?"

"Hell, no, I was going to send for a pizza." He took her hand in his again, linking their fingers. "Some people consider pizza to be an aphrodisiac, did you know that?"

Suspiciously Samantha said, "What people?"

"Mostly members of my family," he retorted, his grin starting again. "What do you say?"

Feeling bràve, Samantha smiled. "I could eat pizza while I read, couldn't I?"

"Samantha—" he protested.

But Henry Boswell returned at that moment with a sheaf of papers stuffed into a fresh manila envelope. He pressed the package into Samantha's hands, saying it was the best they could do under such short notice. She accepted it graciously, thanking Abel's superior and allowing herself to be dragged once again into the corridor.

After them, Boswell called, "I want that report pronto, Fletcher!"

Under his breath, Abel muttered, "Paper pusher."

"If he wasn't around to do his job, you couldn't do yours," Samantha chided. "You're just upset because he called you names."

Abel laughed. "I deserve most of 'em."

When he had deposited her in the passenger seat of his car again, he drove her across the Potomac from Washington to the Virginia city of Alexandria, a place that had been carefully preserved so that parts of it looked like a town from another century. It was a lovely community, especially at nightfall with the streetlamps glowing and candles burning in the windows of some of the old houses.

Abel's home was a small, very pretty stone house in Old Alexandria not far from the birthplace of "Light

Horse" Harry Lee, the Revolutionary War hero and
father of Robert E. Lee. Like most of the surrounding
buildings, Abel's house sported a plaque outside to
announce that it had historical significance. The bot-
tle-green shutters and a weathered front door were
striking in the fading evening light.

There was a garage in the rear, but he didn't pull the
car inside. Samantha caught a glimpse of an airplane
wing through a window.

"Planes have always been a hobby of mine," Abel
said, pulling her up the sidewalk. "The museum didn't
want that one, so I'm rebuilding it myself. I'll have it
in the air by next year."

There was a small patch of grass by his back door
and a clump of daylilies beneath the window, but he
was obviously not a gardener. Samantha could see that
Abel's hobbies reflected his character—dashing and
exciting.

An old man in a white T-shirt was leaning out a
neighboring window, and Abel waved to him before
ushering Samantha through the door. His kitchen was
small and not terribly neat. A heap of letters, magazines, and rolled-up newspapers lay on the kitchen table and cascaded onto the floor.

"I haven't been home long enough to go through the
mail," Abel explained, dismissing the mess.

He led her through a narrow hallway with a sloping
hardwood floor to a sunny sitting room that was decorated with a mishmash of odd pieces—a comfort-
able-looking sofa, a good leather wing chair, but also
a cracked wooden airplane propeller, a chunk of stone
column that did service as an end table, and a blown-up
photograph of a leaping ballerina—complete with au-

tograph. There was a thick Persian carpet on the floor, and its colors shone like jewels.

Abel handed Samantha into the sofa. "Okay, you can read here," he said. "Maybe you'll be finished by the time the pizza gets here."

"May I have something to drink?"

"Oh, sure. A beer?"

Samantha smiled. "When in Rome..."

He cocked a finger at her. "Coming right up."

When he had disappeared, Samantha took off her suit jacket, kicked her shoes under the coffee table, and put on her reading glasses. When Abel returned with two bottles of beer, she was already plowing through the pages and pages of information amassed on the subject of federal funding for national museums.

It was interesting reading, but slow going. Samantha was accustomed to cleanly written reports drawn up by diligent young staffers. The material that Sylvie had come up with wasn't so clearly organized. She found herself going back through things over and over again to keep the facts straight in her mind.

Twice she encountered Abel's name. He didn't have much to do with funding, she could see, but he was listed as one of the field curators who did a great deal of spending. She noticed he'd taken trips to such far-away haunts as Turkey, South Africa, China, and an island in the South Pacific. If she understood what she was reading, he was responsible for bringing a great many expensive exhibits to the Smithsonian and other museums around the country. A real-life Indiana Jones.

The pizza came, but Samantha was too caught up in her reading to stop. She munched on a slice of pizza, hardly conscious of Abel nearby. When she finished the last page, she put the folder down and found Abel sitting on the floor by her feet, hunched over a ring bound notebook and licking pizza sauce off his fingers. He had an antique fountain pen in the other hand and wore a pair of tortoiseshell reading glasses that lent a certain professorial air to his otherwise tough guy good looks. Unaware that she observed him, he frowned over the pages he'd spread all over the coffee table.

Samantha tossed the last crust back into the pizza box and licked her own fingers. "What are you doing?"

He looked up startled by the sound of her voice. "Nothing important."

"Your report for Boswell?"

He gave her a wry grin. "Don't tell him I write them myself, okay?"

"Your secret's safe with me. I've been reading about you, you know. Boswell doesn't hate you as much as he pretends. You're listed as a very productive member of the staff—except for a couple of reprimands. Care to tell me about the Turkish masseuse?"

He laughed, pushing his papers aside and reaching for Samantha's stockinged feet. "No, but I'll show you what I learned from her."

Sometime during the last hour he had turned on a radio, and suddenly the room was filled with a gentle saxophone riff—slow and sexy jazz that made Samantha feel like doing almost anything but talk about legislation. Abel proved that he had learned a great deal from the Turkish lady mentioned in his reprimand, and with a sigh, Samantha fell back on the sofa while he worked magic on her pressure points.

"Now that I have you under my power," Abel said, "why don't you tell me about the funding bill?"

She sighed, enjoying the sensations his gentle hands evoked. "A subcommittee is writing some legislation. They're trying to decide how much money is a fair allocation. They'll have hearings next month, but most of the important points will be decided before that."

"How do *you* feel about the important points?"

She smiled lazily. "You expect me to concentrate when you're doing that? It's heaven, Abel." His expert massage was relaxing Samantha from the tips of her toes on up.

He laughed softly at her catlike sigh. "I want to hear what you think."

"About giving tax dollars to museums? I'm against it. Ouch!"

"Just loosening your muscles. Explain yourself. Why are you against it?"

"The Speaker and I feel the same way about government spending. We hate to see money going to projects that don't serve people directly."

"Don't you think museums serve people?"

"Of course they do. But they also get funds from the private sector. Money is hard to come by, and I think tax revenues ought to feed hungry people or give shelter to the homeless. Why spend money showing people how wonderful the space program is when we could be caring for the sick?"

"You can't take care of all the sick and hungry people in the world."

"No, but we can try."

"We ought to nourish people's minds, too, don't you think?"

Samantha tilted her head to look at him. "Through education, of course."

"Museums educate a lot of people, Samantha. Hundreds of school children come through our museum every day." He argued reasonably, never ceasing in his massage, but gradually working his way up past Samantha's ankles to her calves. "Kids learn about the past when they tour the Smithsonian, and I for one hope they'll put that knowledge to good use—changing the future."

"All right, I agree we can't cut off funding completely. I'm only saying that the government shouldn't be in the business of maintaining collections of bizarre insects, for example."

"You'd be surprised where those bizarre collections come in handy. Last year, the police force of a major American city solved a serial killer case by using information the museum kept on file for decades. How many lives were saved through our help?"

"But that's an isolated case."

"Not really. Our offices field dozens of important questions every day. Some of them do involve life or death situations."

Samantha gave him a smile. "You know, you're not a bad lobbyist."

He frowned and released her legs. "I didn't want to be. I'm supposed to be proving that I'm *not* involved in your upcoming legislation. Now you're going to think—"

His smile warmed, and Samantha's heart turned over. She longed to reach out and curl a lock of his dark hair through her fingers. He had managed to turn her muscles to jelly with his massage, but it wasn't just his touch on her feet and legs that made Samantha feel warm and languid.

It was comfortable being here with him—close together and talking about subjects that interested them both. In his own lair, he didn't seem as dangerous as before. But he was every bit as desirable. Even his reading glasses gave Abel an appealing appearance.

The music changed again, turning mellow and sensual. On the floor, Abel moved into a crouch between Samantha's knees. He smoothed his hands up the outside of her skirt, curled them around her backside and pulled her to the edge of the sofa. As if it was the most natural thing in the world, Samantha slipped her arms around his neck. In a moment, they were nose to nose and smiling. And a moment after that, they were kissing.

His mouth was hot and tasted wonderful. His kiss melted Samantha completely. It was slow, tantalizing, and full of promise.

When he broke the kiss, Abel murmured, "I'm in love with you, Samantha."

Samantha's heart began to slam. "Abel, I—"

"I can't help it," he said swiftly. "I know I'm rushing things. Hell, I've never been good at this stuff. It's never happened to me before."

She laughed unsteadily. "That's painfully obvious, Abel."

He caressed her hair softly. "I've been all over the world, Samantha. I've seen just about everything you can imagine. But this—well, it's the first magic I've ever really believed in."

"Why, Abel, you're a romantic after all."

"I feel like a truck driver invited to Cinderella's ball," he growled. "But I can't stay away. I'm bewitched, Samantha."

"Is that so bad?"

With a frustrated laugh, he said, "I hate feeling out of control like this. But at the same time, it's—well, it's intoxicating."

"I feel a little drunk myself," she admitted shyly.

He kissed her for that—long and so softly that Samantha found herself trembling like an autumn leaf.

Abel's whisper rasped in her ear. "You try to be so proper, Miss Wyatt. You want the world to think you're careful and good and smart. But I can feel something else inside you—a different woman who wants to come out."

"I'm beginning to see sides of you that I like, too."

His grin was crooked. "I'm not such a thug?"

"Not all the time. I actually think you've got an intellectual side, Abel Fletcher."

"Don't spread that around, okay?"

"We both have secrets we'd like to keep, don't we? We're not as different as I first thought." She sighed as he caressed her cheek and asked dreamily, "I wonder what brought us together this way?"

"A spell," Abel breathed in her ear. "And I can't tell you how glad I am that it's finally affecting both of us."

"Oh, it is," Samantha whispered, closing her eyes as he trailed kisses down the column of her throat. "It's definitely affecting both of us."

They kissed a while longer, and Abel's knowing hands coaxed Samantha with caresses that elicited tiny gasps of delight. She dared to touch him, too, enjoying the contour of his chest the breadth of his shoulders, the strength in his arms.

Even his voice caused a wonderful shivery reaction. He asked, "Do you know how hard it is for me—not to drag you upstairs this minute?"

"But you won't."

"I won't?"

She touched her fingertips to his mouth, tracing the strong line of his lower lip as if to memorize the shape. "You're a good man, Abel. You try hard to be a bad boy, but you're—well, I trust you."

He was watching her eyes. "You're going to ask me to take you home now, right?"

She smiled ruefully. "Yes, I am. I know how you feel, but I'm just not ready, Abel."

He studied her face and said seriously, "I want to make love to you—right here on the floor."

"It's too soon for me."

"Someday it will be right."

"You'll be the first to know."

Grimly he smiled and got to his feet.

"All right, I'll be a gentleman again. It's hell, but I'll do it." Extending a hand, he helped her up, then found her shoes and helped Samantha on with her coat. He gathered up his keys, slid into his leather jacket, and turned off the lights and the radio.

In a few minutes, they were riding across the Potomac toward Georgetown in Abel's car. Samantha could see the lights of the monuments glowing in the sky, the shining ribbon of the water beneath them. As they neared Samantha's neighborhood, the traffic thinned out to nearly nothing. Like the people of any small conservative town in America, most of her neighbors went home early at night.

They didn't speak. Samantha was comfortable with the silence. She was glad Abel understood her misgivings.

But maybe they were foolish misgivings, Samantha argued with herself. Other women slept with men long before they reached any conclusions about the future. Did she need a commitment for marriage before allowing herself the pleasure she truly longed for? Even Speaker Glendenning seemed to feel Samantha wouldn't suffer in Abel's capable hands.

"Maybe you should take risks once in a while," Samantha said.

"What?"

She blushed, not realizing that she'd spoken aloud. "Don't mind me," she said, embarrassed. "I'm just arguing with myself."

Abel glanced at her in the light of the dashboard. "Which side is winning?"

"I can't tell yet."

But she had a better idea when he'd parked the car, escorted her to the townhouse, and unlocked the front door with her keys. Carly had left the lights on. There was a note taped to the newel post at the bottom of the stairs.

"I've gone home for an early weekend," said the note. "We're making wedding arrangements. See you on Monday. Carly."

Abel was frowning. "You're here alone, then?"

"I guess so. Carly's getting married this summer and the wedding plans are taking up a lot of her time, so—"

"Is there someone you can call to stay with you?"

Samantha smiled. "Abel, this is my home. I don't need a baby-sitter."

"But—"

"But nothing. I'm a grown-up. I can stay here alone."

"I'm going to have a look around first."

"For what? Burglars hiding in the cellar? For heaven's sake—"

"Indulge me." Already heading toward the kitchen, he said over his shoulder, "I'm not going to lose you now, just when I'm starting to make some headway."

He made a thorough search of the house, even dashing up the stairs while Samantha bemusedly tapped her foot in the front hall. When she heard him go into her bedroom, she wondered if he'd see the big vase of roses, which she had moved to her bedside to better enjoy them. Perhaps he'd even notice the single bloom she'd slept with last night. The petals were still scattered across her pillow.

"All clear," he announced, coming downstairs again without remarking on the roses. He said, "I'll call you in an hour to make sure you're safe."

"Thanks for caring," she said, and then was surprised by the automatic words that popped out of her mouth. He *did* care about her—for her safety, her well-being. He'd proven it over and over. He'd even said he was in love with her. What was she so damned afraid of?

He saw something in her expression and took her hand, a knowing smile starting on his mouth. "Can I kiss you good night?"

She should have said no. She should have shown him the door right then. But she didn't. Couldn't.

He was still wearing his glasses, and Samantha reached up and took them off his nose very carefully. Then she set them by the telephone and walked into his arms. She kissed him, knowing she ought to hold something back. But as soon as her pliant lips touched his, she knew she was lost. Abel pulled her tightly to his frame, and Samantha aligned herself so that their bodies clung together. He murmured her name huskily and deepened the kiss. She felt his soul pouring into her—all warm and confident and sexy as hell.

"Oh, Abel," she sighed, when the kiss broke and they were standing with their foreheads together. "This isn't a good idea."

"It's very good," he murmured, tracing a whorling pattern on her cheek with his thumb.

"We should stop."

"All you have to do is say the word."

"It's stuck in my throat." Shaking, Samantha looked up into his face. "You could say it for me."

"Forget it, lady." His smile was unrepentant. "If it were up to me, we'd have been up those stairs a long time ago."

"Will you be careful?"

Suddenly he was very still. "What are you saying?"

Samantha swallowed hard. "Speaker Glendenning said I ought to—to have a fling with you, but he gave me a very fatherly lecture on the virtues of safe sex that I—"

Abel began to laugh. "Is that your last worry? Because if you're finished—"

"Abel!"

He swept Samantha off her feet and into his arms. "Is this what you want?" he asked. "Have you changed your mind? Are we going up to your bed?"

She was trembling hard, but she forced the word out. "Yes."

"You're sure?"

"I can't be afraid of risks forever."

"I'm not a risk, my love. I'm the safest thing you'll ever find."

He did a Rhett Butler two-at-a-time leap up the stairs, carrying Samantha effortlessly along the second floor hall. The door of her bedroom was ajar, but he kicked it open the rest of the way and threaded her through. She could feel his heart slamming in his chest, and though her own pulse began to match that rushing rhythm, it was suddenly terrifying. What had she done? Turned the tiger loose?

Beside the bed, he set her on her feet and attempted to shuck off his jacket while kissing Samantha at the same time. She started giggling against his lips.

"Stop me, slow me down," Abel commanded, his face illuminated only by the shaft of light that slanted from the hallway. "I don't want this to be over too fast."

"You expect me to be the voice of reason?"

"You have been—until now."

"I've lost my head completely. And it's your fault." Samantha helped him with the jacket and turned her attention to the buttons on his shirt. She drew the shirt off his shoulders and tipped a quivering smile up at him. "But slow down, anyway. If I'm going to be crazy for once in my life, I want it to last."

"All right," he said, unbuckling his belt and whipping it through the loops of his jeans. "But let me warn you, Samantha. It may last all night."

Samantha gulped. She felt more vulnerable than she'd ever felt in her life. Abel's dark, flickering gaze seemed to strip her clothes off her body and delve into the secret places without preliminary.

"You're scaring me."

"You're only scared of yourself, I think."

He turned her around to face the antique mirror and stood behind her, clasping Samantha to his strong frame. There was just enough light to see each other clearly. The rest of the room seemed to fade into dusk. Their eyes met in the mirror, and Abel's were half-closed and vibrantly full of desire for her.

In Samantha's ear, he murmured, "How can you be afraid of me? I love you. Watch how much I love you, Samantha."

He undressed her, and Samantha stared at the mirror, fascinated by the sight of a woman she didn't recognize—a woman whose face became suffused with a glow, her green eyes clouded with passion as Abel's agile hands ranged slowly over her body. From behind her, he unfastened all the buttons down the front of her blouse.

Gently he drew the silky garment off and dropped it on the rug. She could feel the crisp texture of the hair on his chest brushing her back and she leaned against him. Her skirt slipped to the floor next. Then he skimmed her panty hose down and Samantha stepped out of them as if hypnotized. She heard the whisper of his zipper and pressed back against his open jeans, unsteadily flattening her palms on the solid muscle of his thighs.

Watching her eyes in the mirror, he unfastened the front clasp of her bra. Then he hesitated for an instant. His hand looked powerful against her pale skin. His expression was hungry as he raked her nearly naked body. Against the filmy fabric of her panties, she could feel his powerful arousal. But he waited—prolonging the moment.

Samantha moaned softly. "Make love to me, Abel."

"Do you want me?"

Her throat was so dry with desire, she could only whisper. "Oh, yes."

His smile grew wicked. "Show me how much."

She smiled, too. Then she covered his hands with her own and made him slip her bra off. Abel made a quiet noise in the back of his throat as her breasts came to light. Slowly Samantha guided his hands with hers—down to the curve of her hips, then back up to her waist, past the ripple of her ribs to her small, erect breasts. Her skin felt feverish under the caresses. She watched mesmerized as her hands and his teased the woman in the mirror. The woman shivered. Her nipples were stiff, her thighs were trembling. She strained toward the roving hands, seeking the touch, begging for more.

"You're beautiful, Samantha," he murmured in her ear, then took the lobe lightly in his teeth. "So responsive. I could take you right now. Can you feel how ready I am?"

Samantha could only nod. Yes, she could feel him—every powerful inch. She tried to turn around in his arms, but Abel stopped her, forcing Samantha to look in the mirror a little longer. "Wait," he said. "I want to watch you. I want to see your eyes."

He stepped back and finished peeling off his clothing. Samantha stood before the mirror, hugging her aching breasts with her tightly crossed arms. She watched his long-limbed, muscled body emerge from the rest of his clothes and longed to whirl around and push him onto the bed. She wanted to touch him and feel him against her, but she waited, her heart beating wildly, her breath coming in quick gulps,

He came back to her and pulled Samantha's arms away so he could see her body in the mirror again. Standing behind her once more, he eased the silky panties down over her thighs. One of his hands crept into the nest where her pulse seemed to be beating hardest. He touched her, and Samantha's breath escaped in a long, shaken sigh.

In her ear, he said softly, "You're ready too, aren't you?"

Her thin laugh quivered. "Very."

"Do you understand how much I feel for you? How much I care what happens between us?"

She tried to think, tried to concentrate on something besides the thrumming tension inside herself. "I think I do. It's very strange—happening so fast—"

"Sometimes fast is good."

"Then let's be quick now," she said. "I can't—oh, Abel!"

He parted her legs with a nudge, and she felt his erection pressing against her. His voice commanded her just as forcefully. "Open your eyes, Samantha."

She tried her best, but it was so difficult. His fiery gaze met hers in the mirror. With his fingertips, he continued to trace agonizing circles that stimulated Samantha until she was nearly writhing in his arms. He held her still and said hoarsely in her ear, "I want you, Samantha. I want to spend every night of the rest of my life doing this to you."

"Please, I—"

"Once I'm inside you, I'll never leave. I'll be part of you until we die."

"Do it now, Abel!"

With a fluid thrust, he pressed closer yet, but not far enough. His flesh was hot against her own, beating with passion.

His voice shook with the effort of control. "I'm going to make you mine, Samantha. You're my mate for life."

She cried out with pleasure. Her body seemed to explode inside. Never had she felt so desired, so much the center of one man's deepest emotion. His voice, his caress, his pounding heart—it all communicated one message to Samantha. She *was* his. Her body knew it, her subconscious mind sang it as a shattering climax ravaged her.

The room swam around Samantha. Only Abel's quick strength saved her from slipping to the floor in a limp heap of raw nerves.

"Darling, don't faint!"

He caught Samantha up just as her legs gave way. Carrying her to the bed, he managed to rip back the covers and deposit her gently on the pillow. She wound her arms around his strong shoulders and wouldn't let go.

"Why, you little sneak," he said, laughing under his breath. "You weren't fainting at all."

"I'm just a little light headed." She drew him down until his chest nestled against her breasts.

"I want you to see stars," he said, seeking her lips with his own.

"Tonight? Now?"

"Every night."

As they kissed, she caressed him—forcing a shudder from the man who had held her so masterfully a moment before. Every fiber of his body was ready for her. At last, he used his teeth to tear open a foil packet he'd brought along. Samantha helped and caressed him after it was in place, causing Abel to bite out a passionate exclamation as he held her head in his hands.

Teasing him, Samantha began to grow even more excited herself. It was hard to decide where her own trembling left off and his began. Abel said her name, but Samantha didn't hear the rest of his words.

When he couldn't stand her attentions another moment, he rolled Samantha firmly onto her back and sank inside her liquid softness without further preliminaries. It felt quick and good, and the sound he made—a fierce, throaty growl at the moment they joined—brought an ache to Samantha's heart. It was a sound of release, of pleasure. A sound of triumph. And she felt exactly the same way. She held him to her breast as he reveled in their union.

He said, "This is where I belong."

I think so, too. Samantha nearly said the words. But she couldn't find her voice.

Then Abel moved inside her, thrusting deeper still until he found the place that made her gasp. When he moved again, she matched the tempo he created— sometimes slow and tantalizing, then escalating to a wild, insatiable rhythm before turning gentle all over again. Abel glided deeply within her, touching Samantha over and over in that same place that sent pleasure reverberating all the way to her throat. She heard herself making a sexy, purring sound as the delicious sensation grew and welled inside her. Soon they were both out of their heads, moving as one being, breathing as one body, crying out with one voice when ecstasy overwhelmed them.

It wasn't over, however. It simply started again. Laughing and loving it, Samantha wound her arms around Abel's strong shoulders and held on for dear life.

Seven

Abel woke before Samantha did and lay in the bed with her, his heart pounding, his breath short.

What the hell had happened?

It had been wonderful, joyous, awesome sex. Squeezing his eyes shut, Abel replayed the memory of their night together. What had they done? What *hadn't* they done? He remembered Samantha with chocolate pudding smeared on her beautiful mouth after a raid on the kitchen. In his mind's eye he saw Samantha slipping into the bathtub at two in the morning, Samantha breathless with exhaustion an hour later, Samantha drifting off to sleep in his arms.

When they'd made love, Abel had looked into those luminous green eyes of hers and seen the unspoken emotion that had brimmed there. She'd almost said the words.

Words that would have scared the hell out of Abel.

A few days ago I was normal, he said to himself, *now what have I done?*

A beautiful, accomplished, powerful, sexy woman was falling in love with him, and the idea panicked Abel.

He tried to disengage himself from her sleepy embrace to slide out of the bed, but his movement awakened her. She shifted against him, her slender body rubbing erotically against his own.

Her voice was whispery soft and sleepy. "Abel?"

He laughed uneasily. "Yes, it's still me."

She snuggled closer. "I'm glad."

He slid his arm around her more securely. "Did you get any sleep?"

"An hour or two."

She blew a drowsy sigh—one so intimate that Abel fervently wished he was a hundred miles away. The first glimmer of sunlight shone through the tall french windows beside her bed. Her bedroom smelled wonderful—the collection of perfumes on her dresser contributed to that, no doubt. He looked around and saw all the things that reflected her personality—the pretty things mixed with the signs of her work—travel mementos, mostly. The belongings of a complicated woman.

Maybe too much woman for him to handle.

The cat yowled plaintively on the other side of the bedroom door.

"That's Peaches," Samantha said. "She's lonesome."

"Or jealous. I seem to remember kicking her out of here last night."

"She's forgiven you." Another sigh, this one sounding contented. "Abel, did we really take a bath together about two in the morning?"

He closed his eyes, remembering every excruciating detail. "Yes, indeed we did."

"Because we made a mess of chocolate pudding in the kitchen?"

"It was delicious."

Her voice dropped another half octave. "So were you."

"I bit you twice. I'm sorry. I got carried away."

"Maybe we should examine your body in case I inflicted a few damages, too."

He laughed and rolled her over. One second he was scared to death, and the next second he felt like making love to her for the rest of the day. Pinning Samantha to the pillow, he kissed her again, savoring the shape of her mouth, the texture of her skin, the lithe strength of her body against his. She wrapped her arms around his shoulders. Her breasts felt wonderfully soft.

"Darling," she murmured, when the kiss broke. Her lips tickled his chest.

And his conscience. Uncomfortably, he said, "Uh, Samantha?"

"Hmm?"

"Samantha, I want you to know..."

She opened her eyes and smiled. "How marvelous last night was?"

"Y—yes," he said.

Her gaze sharpened, and her body stiffened imperceptibly beneath his. "You don't sound enthusiastic."

"Oh, I am! Really, last night was marvelous."

"But?"

"But what? I'm telling the truth," he insisted. "I think we—"

"Come clean, Fletcher," she said, catching handfuls of his hair in her fingers. "What's the matter?"

"Nothing, nothing." It was too soon to try explaining, for the words were still too tangled up inside his head to make sense. But Abel couldn't stop himself. "I'm—well, I can't help thinking what you said before—about rushing into things, and I—"

"Hold it," she interrupted gently. "I haven't asked you to sell your soul, you know."

He gulped. "I would sell it, though. For you, Samantha, I'd do anything."

"What are you trying to say?"

"My feelings haven't changed. But—"

"You're having second thoughts, aren't you?" She released his hair, pushed him away and sat up suddenly—beautifully naked, beautifully angry. "That's what you're mumbling about!"

"I'm not mumbling, I'm trying to—oh, hell. I didn't expect it to be so intense, that's all."

She frowned, folding her arms delicately across her breasts. "Intense?"

"I've never felt like that before—so close to anyone, so out of control, so desperately in love."

"That's bad?"

"It's—well, it's not what I expected."

"What did you expect?"

"Not to feel so—well, so—"

"You're scared!"

The accusation brought Abel into a sitting position as if he'd been jabbed by a spear. "I am not scared!"

"Oh, no? Then why are you so pale?"

His temper began to simmer. "I'm not pale! It's the light in this silly room that—"

"*My room is not silly!*"

She trembled, her mouth quivering so gently at the edges that Abel longed to fold her into his arms again. He reached for her wrist. "I'm sorry. I didn't mean that."

She eluded his grasp and glared at him. "What *did* you mean?"

"I—I—well, I—"

"Up until now, you've been very direct about your feelings," she accused. "Now that you've maneuvered me into bed, I suppose you'd like to leave, is that it?"

"No! I just—dammit, I'm not used to spilling my guts like this, okay? Give me a second to—"

"You *are* afraid!"

"All right, have it your way! I'm afraid! Does that make you happy?"

Her eyes snapped with anger. "What's so frightening? Me?"

"No. Yes. Both of us. What we're doing together!"

"Isn't it a coincidence," she said stiffly, "that you are having misgivings on the morning *after* we've made love."

"I haven't spent the last few days with you just to get one night of great sex! I'm in love with you, dammit. But it's magic."

"You said that last night," she retorted impatiently, "Only then it sounded romantic! Now you say it like it's a curse or something."

"It is, in a way."

A pretty frown creased her brow. "What?"

It was time to come clean. Abel got out of bed to find his pants. In a moment, he returned and sat down beside Samantha. From his pocket, he pulled the magic stone from Kimi Lau.

"This is the cause of everything."

Puzzled, Samantha accepted the stone. She looked at the bit of painted rock in her hands for a long moment. "What is it?"

"A love charm. King Kimimungo gave it to me a few days ago and—"

"King Who?"

"Kimimungo. He's the king of the island where I was working for the last few months. I used a lot of his people to help me dig up the plane I was looking for, and I paid them wages, for which he was very grateful. In return, he gave me this."

"A rock?"

"It's not just a rock. It's a charm."

"A charm," Samantha repeated, amusement creeping into her voice. "A love charm?"

"Exactly! The king used it to get himself sixteen or eighteen wives, not to mention a slew of kids that—"

"Did he think you needed a charm like this, Abel?" she asked smiling.

"No, he was grateful for—look, I'm being serious, Samantha!"

She toppled back onto the pillows, cradling the stone and smiling as she studied the painted figures. "It's funny looking, isn't it? But very nice. How cute."

"*Cute?*"

"For him to give you such a thing." She giggled. "I wonder what made him think you needed it?"

"I didn't need it!"

"Well, you have to admit you've been a confirmed bachelor for a long time. Not that your technique in bed showed lack of practice, of course."

"Samantha, this is no joking matter!"

"Of course not," she said, peeping a smile up at him. "Did having this rock here last night help turn you into such an animal in bed?"

"Samantha!"

She laughed and sat up, winding her arms around his neck once again and pressing a kiss to his cheek. "Oh, Abel, I'm just kidding. For a minute, you frightened me. I thought you were going to say goodbye."

"I can't," he said hoarsely as her nipples brushed tantalizingly across his chest. "The stone won't let me."

She blew a kiss against his ear. "Well, three cheers for the stone, then. Will it let you make love to me again?"

"Maybe we'd better talk first."

"We've talked enough."

"Samantha," he said, weakening as she caressed him, "I don't think you completely understand. The stone is the reason I've been acting the way I have."

"Of course, darling. Touch me here, will you?"

"Samantha, listen, the stone caused me to fall in love with you."

She sat back again, her arms still looped around his shoulders. "What are you talking about?"

"It's true." Earnestly, Abel tried to explain, "The king gave me this stone with a warning that it would make the first woman I touched fall for me. We bumped into each other at the softball game, remember?"

She was frowning again. "I knocked you over."

"Right. Well, that was the moment the magic started."

"Wait a second. Do you mean if you'd bumped into the vice president you might have fallen in love with him instead?"

"No, it only works between one man and one woman."

Her eyes began to blaze again. "Do you mean to tell me, Abel Fletcher, that you chose me that day simply because of some island mumbo jumbo?"

"It's not mumbo jumbo! Believe me, Samantha, I've seen stranger things, but this really works. Why else would I have fallen so hard for you?"

"Why indeed?" she asked, thoroughly steamed. She got up hastily and grabbed a robe that was draped over the foot of the bed.

"Samantha, please don't be angry. I'm only explaining so you'll understand."

"Oh, I understand all right! You have jungle fever!"

"I do not!"

"I should have known it was too good to be true! You're too *chicken* to admit that you're really in love with me!"

"That's ridiculous!"

"Is it?" She yanked the belt tight around her waist and swung on him, the picture of fury. "I wanted to wait—I was too afraid things weren't going to work out between us, but you were determined! So I trusted you! I gave in to my own feelings and made love last night, and now you're telling me that a stupid piece of *rock* is the only reason we're together!"

"Samantha—"

"You can't admit that the time was right for both of us—that we're two people who were just too damn busy for love until now, and we've found each other and it could be good between us! You're too much of a stubborn tough guy to admit that you've got feelings you can't ignore!"

"*I'm* a stubborn tough guy? What about you? You can't even admit that you *like* me very much!"

"Of course I like you! I might even love you—I can't figure out how I feel, that's all. It happened so fast and you—you—oh, damn you, Abel!"

"You do love me," he said.

"No, I don't!" She stamped her foot for emphasis.

"You do. I saw it in your eyes last night. I could feel it this morning when you woke up. I knew it when the first word out of your mouth today was my name."

He reached for her hand and pulled Samantha to the edge of the bed. "You love me a lot," he said. "We were meant for each other."

She stood stiffly before him. "Because a magic rock says so."

"Yes."

"I want you to leave, Abel."

"What?"

She pushed his hands away. "You heard me. Get dressed and get out. If you don't have the guts to admit that you care for me all by yourself, I don't want any part of you."

"Samantha—"

"You may play with bigger toys than all the rest of the boys on the block, but you're still a boy. Until you can admit how you really feel—"

"Please don't do this, Samantha."

"You're a grown man, Abel, with the feelings of a grown man. Those feelings are scary and sometimes they hurt, but you can't ignore them! You can't pretend they don't exist!"

She whirled around and marched into the bathroom with her head held high. That was Samantha, all right—dignified even in defeat. Abel grabbed his clothes and got dressed before she came out again.

He didn't call goodbye through the door, either. He hustled out of her apartment before she came out swinging.

Samantha heard the door close downstairs and slammed out of the bathroom, knowing Abel was gone but needing to see for herself. He had run out!

"That chicken-hearted idiot! He can camp out in deserts and dig up half the jungles in the world, but he can't admit he really cares about me!"

She stormed back and forth on the needlepoint rug, cursing him, cursing herself, cursing whoever came up with the idea of love in the first place. At last, she got dressed in her most prim outfit and headed for work, determined to throw herself into the first project that crossed her desk and forget all about the man who'd turned her life upside down.

Speaker Glendenning met her at the office door, coming from the opposite direction. Samantha was walking so fast she almost didn't see him until they collided.

"Well, Samantha!" The Speaker greeted her heartily. "Don't we look lovely this morning."

"We look terrible," Samantha snapped. "When was the last time you had that suit pressed?"

"When was the last time you had your mouth kissed? Just a few minutes ago? You look as if you spent the night engaged in tumultuous sex, my dear Samantha.''

''I did not!''

The Speaker laughed. ''Don't lie to me, my girl. I can see it in your face. Young Fletcher finally did it, did he?''

''That depends on what you're talking about,'' she said, pushing past her boss. ''If you mean he finally showed his colors, you're right! I hope he rots in hell!''

''Damn you, Oliver, I should wring your neck!''

From behind his microscope, Oliver looked appropriately terrified. ''What have I done?''

Abel slammed his fist on Oliver's desk. ''You could have talked me out of that stone story, but you didn't! Now I've gone ahead and fallen for her, but the magic has backfired!''

Oliver winced. You didn't mention magic to your lady friend, did you?''

''I had to! We couldn't go through the rest of our life together without her knowing the truth!''

''What did she do?'' Oliver inquired with a halfhearted smile. ''Call the nearest mental hospital?''

''She threw me out ! Can you believe it?''

''Are you surprised?''

Abel threw himself into pacing, not listening to Oliver. ''I can't understand it. Last night was so terrific, so perfect—''

''Why are you telling me this?''

''She's a wonderful woman, Oliver. You should have seen her in Henry's office.''

''You took her to see Dr. Boswell?''

"She was so cool—even he was impressed. She's like a queen, Oliver. You can't ruffle her feathers—well, you can, but—"

"I get the picture," said Oliver, picking up a pencil and pointing it at Abel. "Problem is, she thinks you're nuts."

"Actually, she thinks I'm immature. Talk about ridiculous!"

"*Are* you immature?"

"Of course not!" Abel exploded. "I'm suffering normal misgivings, that's all. I've only known her a couple of days! And it's a big step, you know, committing yourself to a woman for the rest of your life—especially since I'm not sure how long the magic will last. That's where you come in."

"Me?" Oliver paled. "Why do I have to get involved?"

"Because you're the only one who can do the research. You're an archeologist, right? Can't you dig up some information about Kimi Lauan love charms?"

"Well," Oliver chewed his pencil thoughtfully, "I might be able to come up with something in six weeks or so—"

"No, no, no! Six weeks isn't good enough. I need to know tonight!"

"Abel, that's insane! I need at least—" Oliver caught sight of Abel's expression and stopped his protest. He sighed and leaned forward on the desk, man-to-man. "Research isn't what you need, Abel. You don't need to learn more about the charm. You need to learn more about yourself. Why don't you find a good head shrinker and—"

"Dammit, Oliver, I need *your* help!"

Oliver nodded resignedly. ''A shrink would prob-ably have you committed. All right, I'll see what I can do. Give me the stone and I'll compare it to the collec-tions we have in the store rooms.''

''Great!'' Abel dug into his pants pocket but found it empty.

Quickly he dug into his jacket pockets for the stone, then systematically searched his pants again. Fear be-gan to dawn as he realized the stone was not where it ought to be.

''Oh, God! I must have left it at Samantha's house!''

''What are you going to do?''

Abel controlled himself, straightened his posture, and gathered his courage. ''I've got to get it back, that's all.''

''You mean you'll have to go see her again? While she's still upset?''

''I can handle it,'' Abel said firmly. Even as he spoke the words, however, he wasn't sure they were true. Facing an angry Samantha was not something he looked forward to. But he would do it. A woman like Samantha came along only once in a lifetime.

''I can't believe I'm putting myself through this,'' he muttered, heading for the door. ''But it's beyond my control.''

Eight

He had to track her down first, which meant telephoning her office and getting a smooth female voice telling him that Miss Wyatt was unavailable until later in the day.

"Where is she?" he demanded.

"I'm not a liberty to say," said the impersonal voice. "May I take a message?"

Abel checked his watch. "Has she gone to lunch yet?"

"I'm not at liberty—"

"Right, right." *Be crafty, Fletcher.* He dropped his voice and endeavored to sound respectable. "This is Senator Muslephemuph," he said, slurring the made-up name. "I was scheduled for an appointment with her, you see, and my secretary mislaid the details. Can you tell me where Miss Wyatt is lunching? And step on it, please. I'm running late."

The voice said briskly, "Let me check, Senator. Ah. Here it is. Oh, dear. There seems to be some mistake, sir. Miss Wyatt is lunching at the Persephone Club."

"The Persephone Club?"

"Yes, sir. You know. The women's club on Pennsylvania Avenue. She wouldn't schedule an appointment with you there, sir."

"Why not?"

"Why, it's a women's club, sir. No men allowed."

Abel hung up. Did Samantha think she could hide from him in some bastion of the female sex? *Think again, Samantha!*

He checked the phone book for the address and took a cab to the Persephone Club. Abel's first guess was right—the place was a big old Victorian building built of stone that looked like it had come from one of the pyramids. Gargoyles leered down from the eaves, and the front door was made of beveled glass thick enough to withstand bullets. Two women who looked like they were entering a Margaret Thatcher look-alike contest came around the corner and marched up the wide front steps.

Abel squared his shoulders and followed them.

But a slim, elegant young man in a tuxedo stopped him in the posh lobby.

"I'm sorry, sir. This club is restricted."

A trio of women sat in a group of club chairs in the lobby nearby and stopped talking when the kid planted himself in front of Abel. The women were holding tea cups and wearing pearls. They looked startled to see Abel in their midst. The kid kept his voice down, as if he was afraid he'd be spanked for speaking up in their presence.

"You'll have to leave, sir."

Abel thought fast. "Leave? Hell, buddy, you just called me and now you want me to get the hell out. What's going on here? You want your toilets fixed or not?"

The kid blushed. "I don't know anything about broken bathroom fixtures."

"Toilets," Abel corrected loudly. "Just show me the restaurant and I'll get to work."

"There aren't any toilets in the dining room," the kid said, getting suspicious. He eyed Abel's clothes—which weren't anything fancy, but they didn't look much like what a plumber might wear either. "Where are your tools?" he asked. "If you're a plumber, you must have tools."

Abel hooked his thumb at the door. "They're out in the truck. Look, pal, I don't need a hard time from you, okay? I gotta get inside this place if I'm going to fix the—"

"Yes, yes. All right, just let me call the manager. Don't move, please." The kid scuttled for the desk and grabbed the telephone.

Abel knew his big chance when he saw it. While the kid dialed, Abel gave a wave to the tea-drinking ladies and headed up the wide, carpeted staircase behind the two Margaret Thatchers. At the top, a huge bowl of flowers sat on a gilded library table, obscuring a gold-framed mirror. An Oriental runner was underfoot. The Persephone Club spared no expense, that was clear.

Not with servants, either. Another eunuch in a tuxedo came out from behind a maître d's desk to allow the Margaret Thatchers through a huge set of double doors with polished brass handles. When he turned around, he looked appalled to see Abel arrive at the top of the steps.

"Sir," he said disapprovingly. "There must be some mistake."

"No mistake," said Abel. "I need to see Samantha Wyatt right away. Emergency."

The maître d' glanced at Abel's leather jacket and khakis with an expression that made Abel wonder fleetingly if he'd spilled Day-Glo paint on himself. Curling his lip, the maître d' said, "What is the nature of the emergency, sir?"

Abel stuck his face down to the eunuch's level. "None of your business, bub. Now tell me where Samantha is or I'll cause a little emergency right here!"

"I cannot let you into the dining room, sir. Men are forbidden."

"Then bring her out here."

"I can't do that, sir. The program has begun."

"Program? What program?"

"The slide show from the women's commune in Nepal, sir."

"The—? Oh, hell, buddy, just slip in there and tell Samantha I need to see her right away!"

"I'm afraid not, sir."

From the sound of raised voices that suddenly drifted up from the lobby, Abel guessed that reinforcements had arrived and he was about to be bodily thrown out of the Persephone Club. He glanced around and spotted another set of stairs leading up. He ignored the maître d's shout of protest and bounded up the steps two at a time.

"Sir! You can't go up there! Sir, wait!"

At the top of the stairs was another set of doors. Abel bolted through and headed down a thickly carpeted hallway that looked like the corridor of a very expensive hotel. A door opened, a woman stepped out, took one look at Abel and screamed. Abel skidded to a stop, spun around and prudently headed in the opposite direction. At the end of the hall was a fire door. He pushed through, found himself in a stairwell and headed upwards.

At the top of the stairs was another door, this one with a sign posted on it. Board of Directors, Security Patrolled, it said.

Patrolled by whom? Abel didn't take time to wonder. He pulled the door opened and dashed inside, finding himself in a dimly lit reception area. He hustled past a Queen Anne secretary desk and down a hallway that was hung with a series of oil paintings of chubby women in diaphanous white nighties.

Halfway down the hall, he stopped dead.

Something growled at him.

A moment later, another dog slipped out of a room and planted itself squarely in Abel's path. It was a sleek black Doberman. Judging by the growl rumbling behind him, Abel figured they were a matched set.

"Nice doggie," he said softly.

More growling.

"What do these women do up here?" he asked. "Do they have guard dogs to look after their bake sale money?"

The Doberman in front of him took a stiff-legged step forward, growling ominously. Its head was down, ears flattened, body tense and ready to spring.

"Sorry," said Abel. "The bake sale crack was uncalled for. Lie down, okay?"

His suggestion was not obeyed. He edged sideways, hating the idea of a slavering dog standing just a few feet from his rear flank. The thought of being bitten in the butt was not appealing at all. Both dogs began to bark when he moved, but he managed to flatten his back against the wall, The dogs confronted him, growling deep in their throats and giving an occasional bark.

"*Shh!* What d'you want to do, get me arrested? Have a heart, guys. If Samantha sees me get arrested in this place, she'll never speak to me again."

The dogs did not listen to reason.

"Sit!" Abel commanded, trying another tack. To his delight, one of the dogs obeyed.

"What are you, a tough guy?" he asked the other dog.

Cautiously Abel felt around in his pocket for something to distract the dogs. His wallet, his handkerchief, and his Swiss Army knife. Thinking fast, he knotted the handkerchief and braced himself for a hell of a run.

"Okay, guys," he said soothingly to his captors. "I'm gonna make a run for that door over there, see? And I want you two to bite my handkerchief, not my legs, got that?"

No sense waiting. Abel seized his courage and bolted, waving the handkerchief behind him as he ran. Both dogs barked and gave chase, one sinking its teeth into the fluttering hankie and yanking it out of Abel's hand. The other dog got a mouthful of Abel's trousers and didn't let go. Abel flung himself through the narrow door and managed to snatch his trousers out of the dog's teeth. The trousers tore with a resounding rip.

But Abel made it through the door alone, and he leaned thankfully against the door while the dogs went crazy on the other side.

There was no time to linger, of course. He hotfooted his way through a labyrinth of smaller rooms—

storage and maintenance, mostly, he decided. Then he spotted a sign posted on another door and stopped short. It said, dining room.

"Terrific," Abel said. He let himself through the door and was immediately standing in total darkness. After a minute, his eyes got accustomed to the light, and he decided he was standing on a kind of balcony. He could hear a microphoned female voice droning somewhere beneath him, so he edged to the balcony railing and pushed aside a heavy velvet curtain.

The club dining room lay below, and it was the size of a ballroom. A slide show was in progress, and by the dim light of the projector, Abel could make out the scene. Round tables filled with ladies were scattered around the room—only about half of them full.

"Not many people interested in communes in Nepal, eh?" Abel muttered.

He couldn't find Samantha in the crowd. He leaned farther over the railing to get a better view but suddenly heard a commotion behind himself. A barking dog and a raised human voice told him that someone was still in hot pursuit. He looked around quickly for an escape route, but there was no way out.

He was trapped. There were two choices—capture and certain arrest by the club employees, in which case he might never see Samantha again. Or a leap into the ballroom, which could result in broken legs at worst, certain humiliation at best.

"What the hell," he said. "How can I be more humiliated than I am already?"

The doorknob to the balcony was suddenly rattled from outside. Abel threw one of his legs over the balcony railing and measured the distance to the chandelier with his eye. As the door opened and two growling

Dobermans hurled themselves at him, Abel made his leap.

Samantha was calmly watching some lovely scenic slides of a distant, snowy country and wondering if she could get there by cruise ship, when suddenly the Persephone Club's weekly travel luncheon was interrupted by a terrible ruckus from above.

"What in the *world*?"

She heard a shout, dogs barking, then a scream from a woman sitting at the next table. The slide projectionist juggled the light suddenly, sending a picture of a woolly yak careening over the wall. In the next second, the light flashed on, and one of three priceless crystal chandeliers overhead swung crazily.

"No," said Samantha, rising instinctively to her feet. "It can't be."

But it was. Like Errol Flynn, a tall, agile male figure swung from the chandelier by one arm. He could have dropped to the center table quite gracefully at that moment, but suddenly the chandelier's mooring gave way, and the whole thing came crashing down. Women shrieked and leaped back from the table as it smashed under the weight of the chandelier and one very red-faced Abel Fletcher.

He landed on his feet, though, and shouted, "Don't be alarmed, ladies. Just a routine inspection!"

Nobody believed that, of course. One woman swung her purse and hit Abel across the shoulder. He ducked and someone else threw a glass of water in his face. Half the water landed on a visiting congresswoman, however, who cried out and instinctively hurled her dessert back at him. Abel twisted, the orange sherbet bounced off his sleeve and landed in the hair of another woman. A waiter who'd been clearing the tables tried to get out of Abel's way, but Abel hit the man's tray, which went flying, spraying dirty dishes and glassware in every direction.

From the balcony above, a voice shouted, "Grab that man!"

Everybody immediately stepped back, giving Abel a chance to escape. But he didn't take it. He looked around. "Samantha!"

She stepped over the rubble of the chandelier and crushed table and into the limelight. Looking up at the balcony, she called to the club manager, "Marcel! I thought we scheduled this security drill for *next* week!"

Hanging over the balcony railing, Marcel looked mystified. "What?"

But Abel was quicker on the uptake. "Your system is woefully out of date, Marcel," he called. "You'll get my report *and* my bill in the morning!"

"Don't press your luck," Samantha muttered to him, grabbing Abel's arm and steering him purposefully through the throng of astonished diners. She made an effort to smile disarmingly and said gaily to the women around her, "You know Marcel! We have to keep him on his toes!"

She hustled Abel out of the dining room and into the hallway outside. Then her temper boiled over.

"Just what do you think you're doing here?"

"I came to see you."

"This is a private club! You can't just barge in here and play Tarzan when you get the urge!"

"That was a mistake. I had no choice. I knew I'd get arrested, but I had to see you—"

"You may still get arrested!"

He was smiling, damn him.

"I don't think so," he said. "You protected me in there. And you were pretty quick on your feet, love. I admire a woman who can think fast and act—"

"Stop it" Samantha commanded. "You are not my knight on a white charger! You just wrecked a priceless chandelier!"

With a grin, he said, "I've always wanted to do the Douglas Fairbanks routine."

"Damn you, Abel—"

"I know, I know. I'll pay for it—every penny, I promise. I could have gotten in here a lot easier if I'd rented a monkey suit and pretended to be a waiter. Where do you get those guys, anyway? A harem supply store? What a bunch of wimps!"

"They're civilized gentlemen who respect the wishes of the women who own this club—which is more than I can say for you!"

Abel's expression turned earnest. "I respect you, Samantha. Lord, I *love* you!"

"Don't say that!" She clapped her hands over her ears.

"Why not? It's the truth. I do love you, Samantha."

"I don't believe that, Abel. Not after what you told me this morning."

"I know it's hard to understand," he rushed to say. "The stone isn't what you're used to. If you'd been doing my job for twenty years, it wouldn't be so difficult to believe, but—"

"Listen, Abel, I think you've been playing without a helmet too long."

"I'm not crazy!"

"Then you're a little boy who won't take responsibility for your feelings! We can't always control our emotions, Abel. Lord knows I can't! But—"

"What does that mean?"

"What does what mean?"

"That you can't control your feelings. Does that mean you care for me?"

Flustered, Samantha cried, "You know I do! I just can't—"

He seized her by her shoulders, his eyes blazing. "Are you falling in love with me, Samantha? Just a little bit?"

"How can I help it?" she demanded. "You're so—so blasted *silly* sometimes that it just shows you're not the caveman you pretend to be!"

His hands gripped her hard with excitement. "Darling, I know we can make this work. I love you so much—"

"No, you don't," Samantha said sharply.

"Of course I do!"

"I don't believe you," she said shortly. "And until you can make me believe those words, don't say them to me anymore."

Abel stared at her. "What more can I do, Samantha? I've made love to you already—surely that shows—"

"I want you to get rid of that stone," she said.

Abel released her abruptly. "What?"

The magic stone was in Samantha's jacket pocket. She pulled it out and held the painted trinket on the palm of her hand. "I want you to throw this away or give it to your best friend or—oh, I don't care what happens to it. I just won't base a relationship on your belief in this—this—"

"It's a love charm."

"It's a useless stone, Abel!"

"It's magic!"

"Break the magic." Samantha pushed it into Abel's hand. "Break the magic, and we'll see if you feel the same way about me."

When Abel accepted the stone, Samantha realized how hard she was trembling. She was used to giving ultimatums, but not the kind on which the rest of her life depended. Watching Abel's expression cloud with doubt, she suddenly wanted to snatch back the stone. She didn't care why he loved her—not really! The love was enough all by itself.

But a more sensible part of her personality took over—the cool executive, the cautious woman who guarded her heart with a prickly shield of armor.

"Until that stone is gone," she said, her voice quivering, "I don't want to see you, Abel."

He blinked. Then, hoarsely, he said, "I want you more than anything I've ever wanted in my life, Samantha."

There wasn't time for more. Samantha could hear Marcel and his group of security guards tramping down the stairs. But Abel cupped her face in his hands anyway, gazing intently at her as if to memorize every detail. In his eyes, she read terrible emotions—anger and frustration that battled with the love reflected there. Then he kissed her lightly, his lips warm and his hands gentle but firm on her face.

A second later, he was gone, dashing down the stairs just ahead of Marcel's baying pack, leaving Samantha shaken and numb. Suddenly she had tears in her eyes, and something inside her died a little. What had she done?

For a second, she wanted to run after him. But she stopped herself.

She made her way back to the office somehow—a cab and an unsteady walk from the street. Over and over again, she asked herself the same question. "Have I ruined everything?"

Speaker Glendenning burst into Samantha's office several hours later. "Holy Ghost!" he harrumphed. "Why is it so dark in here?"

Coming out of her reverie, Samantha reached forward and snapped on the lamp on her desk. "Sorry," she mumbled, blinking as the light filled her quiet room. "I have a headache."

"That's a lie." The Speaker deposited his heavy frame into a spare chair and eyed his assistant from across her desk. "They tell me you've been locked in your office all day, not taking phone calls so you could work on a report. What report?"

"Report? Oh—Uhm, well—"

"You're not working on any damn report are you?" the Speaker demanded triumphantly. "You're sitting in here by yourself moping!"

"I do not mope!"

"Oh, no?" Glendenning leaned forward and studied Samantha shrewdly. "I think you've just made a big mistake and you're regretting it. And don't tell me you don't make mistakes!"

"Not often," Samantha snapped.

"But this time?"

She sighed and found she couldn't answer. Avoiding her boss's searching gaze, she turned her face away.

"I know that look," the Speaker said.

"What look?"

"A certain faraway expression that says you're arguing with yourself."

"Surely that's better than arguing with you."

He shrugged. "Maybe not. I think you're in conflict with yourself, Samantha. Does it have to do with a certain dashing fellow from a museum?"

"He is not dashing!"

With a sigh, Glendenning asked, "Samantha, honey, can I give you some advice?"

Feeling absurdly grumpy, she said, "As long as I'm free to ignore it."

"Fair enough. Here it is: Don't let pride stand in the way of your happiness."

"Pride?" Samantha was astonished. She sat up in her chair and planted her elbows on the desk. "Is that what you think I'm doing?"

"I think it's likely." More kindly, the Speaker said, "Honey, some people feel like they've always got to be the boss. Usually it's a strong person—like me, like you, like Fletcher. We feel like we've got to be in charge."

"What's wrong with that?"

"Nothing. As long as you don't feel you have to beat somebody to get what you want. That goes in politics as much as in love. You can't break people's spirits—you only kill things that way."

Samantha chewed on her lower lip for a while. "Am I trying to break Abel?"

"Only you can answer that." Looking almost grandfatherly, the Speaker said, "I only know you've got to give a little sometimes, if you want to win. That's the way politics work, right?"

Samantha considered the Speaker's words. Slowly, she said, "I don't think it's possible to break Abel Fletcher's spirit."

Glendenning smiled. "I agree with you. But you can chase him away, if you try hard enough."

Samantha thought for another moment, surprising herself with a quick solution. "Sir?"

"Yes, honey?"

"May I take the rest of the day off?"

With a chuckle, the Speaker rose to his feet. "Take as much time as you need, Samantha. We'll muddle along without you somehow."

"Thanks," she replied, getting up and preparing to leave. "I think I've got some business to take care of."

"Go for it!"

Samantha entered the Smithsonian uncertainly, armed with Abel's office number. Her head had been filling with thoughts of him alone, and setting foot in his domain was oddly comforting.

She had been in the Smithsonian before, of course. Its vast halls contained some of the most extraordinary exhibits Samantha had ever seen. But as she entered the castle this time, her thoughts did not concern the largest gems, the collections of stuffed animals, or famous documents. This was Abel's domain, a place where he had put his mark on the world.

Perhaps her work affected the lives of the people she worked for, but Abel had contributed to the accomplishments of other scientists in a way that would be viewed and remembered for generations to come. It was a daunting thought—one that filled Samantha with respect.

After asking for directions, Samantha found herself heading down a dark staircase to a dim hallway lined with office doors. The recorded music of Indian tom-toms emanated from one of the rooms. Through the open doorway of another office, Samantha glimpsed the skeletal remains of some monkeylike creature.

She found Abel's office and knocked hesitantly on the door. Her heart pounded in her chest.

Suddenly the door was snatched open from within. "Thank heaven you're back!" said a strange voice. "For a while, I thought you'd really—oh. Who are you?"

"My name is Samantha Wyatt. I'm looking for Abel Fletcher."

He was a young man with wildly curly hair that was just barely contained in a ponytail. His lab coat was decorated by a button that read, "Life is like a bowl of granola. Mostly nuts and flakes."

He stared at Samantha as if she'd just landed from the planet Mars. "So you're the one."

"The one?"

"Yeah, the woman he flipped for."

Somewhat bitterly, Samantha said, "To hear Abel tell it, a stone is the reason he flipped."

"I don't believe that for a second," said the young man, looking at her sideways. "Do you?"

Samantha decided not to answer that one. "Who are you, may I ask?"

"Oh!" He grinned and opened the door wider. "I'm Oliver Andrews. I work with Abel sometimes. That's why I'm here. This is his office. I'm doing some research for him."

"I see. Is Abel here?"

"No, I thought maybe you—well, when I heard someone in the hall I thought he had come back."

"Come back? Where did he go?"

Oliver looked at her for a second and sighed. "Maybe you'd better come in and sit down."

Her curiosity alive, Samantha entered the long, narrow office. She couldn't suppress a smile as she looked at Abel's things—the books, journals, bits of old airplanes mixed with rock and roll posters, and vintage photographs. Even more than his house had reflected his character, Abel's office seemed to define the man— a little serious scholarship blended with a fun-loving side that was irrepressible.

Suddenly she longed to be with him, and she turned to his colleague eagerly. "Oliver, I—I have to talk to Abel. Can you tell me where I can find him?"

"Kimi Lau."

"Who?"

Oliver laughed. "It's not a who, it's a where. It's a place, an island."

Blankly, Samantha said, "He's gone to an island?"

"Yep, in the South Pacific. It's the place where he got the rock from King Kimimungo. You know about the crazy rock, right?"

"It's not a rock, it's a love charm," Samantha said sharply, feeling ridiculously defensive. "Why did Abel go back there?"

"To end the spell, he said."

"To—?"

"To give the rock back. And believe me," Oliver said heavily, "It's not going to be as easy as it sounds."

"Why?" Anxious suddenly, Samantha asked, "Is Abel in any danger?"

"Heaps," said Oliver. "I told him he was to old for that kind of stuff, but he wouldn't listen to me. He's going to go through the ceremony."

"What kind of ceremony is it?"

"Well," Oliver began, his eyes bright as he plunged into the details of Abel's expedition, "first he had to swim out to this little volcano, you see—"

"A volcano!"

"It's been inactive for years," Oliver assured her, "but then there's a test of strength and endurance that—"

"Wait," Samantha said firmly. "You mean Abel could really get hurt?"

"You bet, " said Oliver. "He's too old for the kind of thing he's heading for on Kimi Lau."

Samantha grabbed Oliver's arm. "Come on," she said. "You can explain the rest to me in a cab."

"Why? Where are we going?"

"To the airport. I've got to catch him before he gets on the plane!"

Oliver resisted. "You can't catch him. Abel flew himself. If you want to follow, you'll have to get on a commercial flight to Kimi Lau."

Samantha gulped. "I—I have to fly?"

With a grin, Oliver said, "Unless you can swim a couple of thousand miles, the only way to catch Abel is to buy a plane ticket and get into the air."

"Oh, damn."

Nine

Samantha called her office to announce that she'd be taking a few days off.

"Are you sick?" asked her secretary.

"Lovesick, maybe," Samantha muttered before saying goodbye.

She spent the rest of the day making preparations for the trip to Kimi Lau. The first flight she could catch didn't leave until nine the following morning. Samantha slept badly that night. More than anything in the world, she hated flying.

On Friday morning at the appointed hour, Samantha arrived at National Airport to board her plane. According to Oliver's instructions, she was dressed in jeans, sneakers, and a cotton shirt and had brought along a heavy sweater and windbreaker. She carried a canvas shoulder bag, too, which Oliver eyed curiously when he met her at the gate.

When the security guard waved her through, Oliver said, "What's in the bag?"

"A few things I thought Abel and I might need."

"A first aid kit, you mean?"

"Not exactly."

Oliver took a closer look at Samantha's face. "You look a little green this morning, Miss Wyatt. Are you sure you should make this trip?"

"I'll be okay," Samantha said faintly. Then, "Just make sure I get on the plane, Oliver. Don't let me chicken out."

"You're having second thoughts?"

Samantha shook her head, not willing to explain her dislike of flying. "Just ignore me if I start babbling like a terrified baboon, all right?"

"You got it, Miss Wyatt."

She took a deep breath. "Here goes nothing."

On Kimi Lau, Abel found the king's interpreter, the native he had come to think of as Mickey Rooney. Outside Mickey's beachside grass hut, which was equipped with a satellite dish and two children who made faces at Abel through an open window, Mickey solemnly listened to Abel's story.

"Okay," he said at last. "I take you to love god's cave. Cost you fifty bucks, man."

"Fifty!"

Mickey shrugged. "Okay, forty, but that's cash. No American Express."

Abel counted out the bills quickly. "When do we leave?"

"Right now soon enough?"

Abel looked at the ocean just a few hundred yards from Mickey's hut. The surf rolled onto the white beach in huge waves, crashing noisily on the beautiful white sand. Hanging low in the sky, the late afternoon sun glistened on the water, making a picturesque scene suitable for postcards. Only it was the kind of scene that made Abel want to throw up.

He said, "I don't suppose there's another way to get to the god's cave besides by canoe?"

Mickey grinned. "Only if you can fly, man. Why? You got a problem with my canoe?"

"It's not that," Abel said, unwilling to admit how much he hated riding in tippy little boats on open water. He wasn't big on swimming either—he preferred to do it in swimming pools, not bottomless oceans teaming with man-eating wildlife. He'd flown himself across country, then taken a commercial flight to one of the big islands and hopped a helicopter ride to Kimi Lau that afternoon. He had hoped to get a good nights' rest before embarking on a gut-wrenching canoe ride.

"What do you say, man?" Mickey asked impatiently. "Go now or not? *Santa Barbara* comes on in an hour. I don't miss that for nobody, man."

"Okay, okay," Abel said, swallowing manfully. "Let's go."

Mickey's canoe turned out to be everything Abel despised in a boat. It was old, it leaked, it had little sharks painted on the side, and there were no life jackets.

His face must have been pale as he stood on the hot sand staring down at the craft, because Mickey suddenly said, "Why you want to do this so bad, man? Why don't you just buy some postcards and go home again?"

"I've got to do it," Abel said glumly. "My life depends on it."

"Your life, man?"

He sighed. "I'm starting to think of her that way."

"Her? What's going on here?"

"It's partly your fault," Abel growled, finally working up some anger. "If your buddy the king hadn't given me this lousy charm, I'd be a different man today!"

Mickey's English didn't extend as far as colloquialisms, and he looked puzzled, then defensive as soon as Abel pulled the painted stone out of his pocket. "Whoa! No money-back guarantees on love charms, man. That one not work so good? You want another? You give me ten bucks, I get you another."

"Good Lord, I don't want *another* one, you idiot! This one was bad enough! I—wait a second. I thought this stone was passed down through the king's family."

"Right, right," Mickey said hastily. "Many generations. Lots of big magic."

Unhappily Abel glared at the stone in his hand. "But I want to break the magic now, so let's get on with it."

Gathering his courage, Abel climbed into Mickey's canoe and settled himself rigidly in the front seat, grabbing the gunwales of the little boat and hanging on for dear life. "No hotdogging, you hear?" he yelled at Mickey over the thunder of the surf. "Just paddle me out there and drop me off!"

Then Abel stifled a yelp of fear as Mickey launched the canoe onto the ocean. The little craft rocked crazily in the surf for a second, then Mickey hopped aboard and started paddling like mad.

Abel forced himself not to look at the water and occupied his brain with travelogue facts. A heap of rocks off the southernmost beach of Kimi Lau had been called the Nest of the Love God for centuries, as far as Abel knew. Very few plants grew on the rocks—just a few palm trees and clumps of grass. It was not large enough to be an island yet, for a small hurricane could submerge all five hundred yards of its coastline.

The rocks were the result of an undersea volcano that hadn't erupted for twenty-five years. The natives didn't live on the island because nobody could grow food on it, and it was too treacherous for most tourists to clamber over. But the main feature of the little clump of real estate was its underground cave.

"Tell me about the cave," Abel yelled at Mickey, to take his mind off the unpleasant rocking of the canoe. His face was wet with ocean spray—or his own terror-induced perspiration.

"Very beautiful cave!" Mickey called back, paddling expertly over the waves. "But dangerous, too, y'know? Stories say the man who throws back the magic love charm maybe lose his life in the cave. Maybe the love god get mad and blow up again, you know?"

"The volcano, you mean?"

"That's what stories say, man. You be careful in there. But then, you're big, brave American guy. You can handle it, right?"

"Right," said Abel, hoping he sounded sure of himself. He closed his eyes for the rest of the trip across the waves.

Mickey landed his canoe on the rocky shore of the tiny island and hopped out into knee-deep water. He dragged the canoe up onto the rocks. Abel climbed out nimbly, glad to have solid ground under his feet.

Feeling like a new man, he looked around with interest. "This is the place, eh?"

"You bet, man. Cave is down that way, see?"

Abel strode over the rocky terrain. The island was made of lava rock that crunched under his boots. Spotting a cleft in the stone, he cut directly to that spot and found himself standing at the top of some stone steps that had been cut by men. At the bottom of the steps, he could see a glimmer of water.

"Nest of the Love God," Mickey said. "Sometimes couples come out here for hanky-panky, you know? Stories say it's a good place to make babies. We let you have it sometime, man. Fifty bucks a night. We even bring you wine coolers."

Abel frowned at his entrepreneurial sidekick. "You people certainly know how to turn a dollar."

Mickey shrugged guilelessly. "You gotta take advantage of the opportunities. Listen, I'd love to stick around, but I got that show to watch, you know, so I'll be back for you later, okay?"

"How much later?"

"Hour and a half," said Mickey, who then grinned. "Unless I hear you're dead first."

"Everybody's a comedian."

When Mickey was back in his canoe and industriously paddling away to watch his soap opera, Abel took courage in hand and went down the steps to the cave.

What he found was more of a grotto than a real cave, and he could see evidence that the place had once been the site of a volcanic eruption. The lava had simply settled in a way that formed an underground chamber.

Cautiously descending the steps, Abel entered and looked around. The grotto was perhaps thirty feet across and twice that distance in length. The lava floor had cooled in an undulating formation, sloping gently downward, then disappearing into a seemingly bottomless hole. The mouth of the hole appeared to be about the size of a Volkswagon Beetle in diameter. Some safety-minded Kimi Lauan had built a wooden railing to prevent a stupid tourist from falling into the hole.

A shining pool of water lay in the nearest corner of the cave. It was bright green and very clear. A soft mist hung in the air over it. Someone with a vivid imagination might expect to see the gleaming head of a primordial serpent rise from the depths—or perhaps flashes of flame licking from the cracks in the walls around the pool. Rhythmic sounds of the ocean echoed quietly in the chamber.

There had to be at least one other entrance to the cave, Abel noted, for shafts of fading sunlight penetrated the jagged walls, creating eerie patches of light. The pool of water seemed to be illuminated from inside itself, in fact. If Oliver's research was correct, the water was believed by the island natives to have healing powers.

Impulsively Abel crouched and plunged his fingers into the pool. He was surprised to discover how warm the water was as it caressed his skin. Even more surprising was his discovery that it was freshwater, not salty. No wonder native couples came to frolic in this natural hot tub.

He stood up and dried his hand on his trousers. "No sense putting this off, Fletcher."

From his pocket, Abel took the smooth stone that King Kimimungo had given him. It seemed like a long time ago. As he stared at the oddly erotic figures painted on the stone, he couldn't help thinking about his night of love with Samantha.

He sighed harshly. "There won't be any more nights like that," he said aloud. "Not until you get rid of this stone and start acting like a normal man."

Closing his fist, he hefted the stone in his hand.

"This better work," he muttered.

He climbed to the top of an altarlike rock formation, slipping once, but regaining his balance easily. At the top, he found solid footing. Then, winding up and closing his eyes for good luck, he pitched the stone into the yawning hole at the bottom of the cave.

Except that he blew it. The stone bounced once, and Abel opened his eyes in time to see his damned love charm end up sitting on the tip of a stalagmite.

"Dammit!"

There it sat, on the other side of the wooden railing, mocking him. It was as though the blasted thing refused to die.

"Now what am I supposed to do?"

The answer was obvious, of course. He had to get down, climb over the railing and retrieve the stone so he could throw it all over again.

His boots slithered on the lava rock as he climbed down off the altar. Muttering, Abel jerked off his jacket and dropped it on the grotto floor before swinging his legs over the wooden railing, which wobbled under his weight.

"This is what Oliver was talking about when he mentioned dangerous," Abel said. "Except this is my own damn fault. I could have thrown it straight the first time."

He scrambled down the steep slope toward the stalagmite.

Suddenly a weird phenomenon took place. For a fleeting second, Abel thought he was experiencing a volcano rumble. The floor trembled under his feet. The air was suddenly pungent with the odor of sulfur. A soft, steady roar filled his ears, starting as a quiet vibration and building to a chest-tingling thunder.

At that moment, Abel lost his balance and slipped.

He cursed, flinging his arms wide to regain his footing, but to no avail. He fell hard, the breath leaving his body in one great whoosh. Instinctively he grabbed for a handhold in the hard lava rock. It was no use. He began to slide toward the rumbling maw of the cave.

He shouted once, then began to curse steadily as he slid downward, frantically grabbing for anything that could stop his plunge. His fingernails scratched uselessly at the rock.

Then, miraculously, his left boot found a toehold, and his whole body jammed to a halt. Panting, he hung there. The rock vibrated against this cheek, and the steady rumble of eruption echoed in his ears.

"Okay, hotshot," he said to himself. "Now what?"

Mickey wasn't due back for hours. In the meantime, Abel knew he could slide into the bottomless pit or be blown off the face of the earth by a volcano. Other options weren't very plentiful.

Then a voice above him said, "Darling, what are you doing down there?"

Abel jerked his head to look and almost lost his toehold when he saw the face that leaned down over the railing. "Samantha? *Samantha!*"

"Are you in trouble?"

He tried not to pant. "Of course not!"

She looked beautifully mystified, and Abel had never been so happy to see anyone in his life. For a second, he wondered if he was dreaming, but she said, "Abel, that looks very dangerous."

He laughed breathlessly. "Oh, this is kid stuff. Wait til you see what I do for an encore!"

She laughed, too, a wonderfully musical sound in the cave. "Oh, Abel you're the only man I know who swings from chandeliers and scampers around volcanoes!"

Volcanoes. "Samantha, you've got to get out of here."

"But I came to see you. To talk to you."

"Well, you're thirty seconds too late. Now scram before this whole place blows sky-high!" He peered upward again to see if she was listening to his orders.

Dressed in a lovely cruise ensemble that undoubtedly cost a small fortune, she blinked and frowned. "Before it blows sky-high?"

"The volcano! Can't you hear it?"

"Oh, you mean that roaring sound! Abel, that's not a volcano eruption."

"What?"

As he painfully hung on for dear life, Samantha pulled from her handbag what appeared to be a pocket travel guide. She steadied her sunglasses on top of her head and flipped through the pages, frowning delicately. "Let's see—ah, here it is. 'The Nest of the Love God is also the site of an unusual freshwater geyser. The eruptions of the geyser take place when the high tide and the—"

"Hold it! You mean this thing is going to spew water all over—"

He didn't get a chance to finish. At that very instant, the rumbling beneath him suddenly increased to a roar. A belching gurgle preceded an enormous blast of hot water that instantly soaked Abel to the skin. He held his breath as the gush blasted past him. In another instant, the rock to which he clung to perilously turned as slick as a snowy driveway in January.

The geyser only lasted half a minute. But to Abel, it felt like two decades. He tried not to whimper as he hung onto the lava and rivulets of water streamed past him and back down into the hole. He didn't dare move a muscle.

Above him, Samantha's enraptured voice said, "Oh, wasn't that breathtaking! Abel, I never thought I'd admit it, but your work is so much more exciting than mine."

Abel ground his teeth and forced his voice not to sound panicky. "Samantha, love, I don't suppose you brought anybody with you?"

"No," she said, "I felt we needed to be alone, Abel. There's so much I want to tell you. Won't you come up so we can talk face-to-face?"

Abel didn't dare crane his head to look up at her. He felt his toehold growing less secure by the moment and gulped back terror. "Darling," he said, "would I be blowing my image if I asked you for a teeny bit of help here?"

"Oh, I'd love to help! What are you doing, exactly?"

"At the moment," he said breathlessly, "I'd just like to get back up there with you."

She sighed. "You really can be romantic when you want to be."

"Have you got some rope, by any chance?"

"N—no," she said, sounding doubtful. "Why?"

"Is there anything around up there that you could lower to me? A ladder in the corner? Anything?"

"Abel, are you really in trouble?"

"Of course not. I just can't seem to—"

Her voice sharpened. "Because it looks very dangerous, you know."

"Are you wearing a belt, Samantha?"

"Why, yes."

"Take it off."

She must have obeyed and figured out what came next, because her belt soon appeared in front of Abel's nose. He made a grab for it and thankfully wrapped it once around his hand. "Anchor yourself against something, okay? I don't want to pull you down here, too."

"Right," she said briskly. "Ready!"

He risked a glance up at her and saw Samantha teetering at the top, one leg wrapped around the base of the wooden railing to secure herself while she leaned precariously down toward Abel. Her color was high, and her hair blew attractively around her face. Abel grinned. She had guts, all right.

"What are you smiling about?" she demanded. "This looks very scary to me."

"Not from this angle," Abel said gallantly. "You're a hell of a woman, Samantha."

She grinned. "Come up here and say that."

Gamely Abel tried his weight on the belt and decided that Samantha just might be capable of preventing him from sliding into the mouth of hell. He said, "I'm going to pull myself up now. Yell if you feel yourself slipping."

"I'm fine," she said, though her voice was tight with exertion.

Cautiously Abel began to haul himself upward. It was slow going, and once his foot slipped, sending a shower of rock bits down into the geyser. Samantha gasped but didn't let go.

"Good girl," he coached. "Just one more second—"

She grabbed his free arm and used her weight to haul Abel up over the lip of the geyser's edge. Together they sprawled back on the lava rock, panting and laughing at the same time.

Abel sat up first, his heart still pounding in his chest. "Lady," he said, "you're one of a kind. Will you marry me?"

Ten

———

Samantha tried not to lose her head. She propped herself up on her elbow and said, "We need to talk, Abel."

He crawled across the last few inches between them and pinned Samantha to the floor of the cave. His clothes were soaked, but she could feel the heat of his body and enjoyed the naturally intimate way he fit against her. He said, "So talk. You can start with what the hell you're doing here."

Her heart was hammering, but she managed to stay outwardly calm. "Isn't it obvious? I came to be with you."

"That's a lie," he said, a grin playing on his sensual mouth. "You thought you had to rescue me, didn't you?"

"Certainly not! I—"

"My manly pride can take it. You don't have to treat me like I'll fall apart."

"All right," she said uneasily, letting her hands trail to the firm contour of his shoulders. "I'll admit I was a little worried about you. Oliver said you'd come tearing over here to get rid of the stone. I was afraid I had sent you into something dangerous."

"As you can see, I'm perfectly safe."

"Yes, but—"

"But nothing," he overrode her next question quickly. "You conveniently came along to help me out of that little jam."

"Little jam! Abel, tell the truth. Were you—"

"Forget about me. You didn't have to come all the way to Kimi Lau to check on my health. You could have made a phone call for that, but you jumped on a plane instead. And if I remember correctly, you're not crazy about flying."

She swallowed with difficulty. "Maybe not. But...I wanted to be sure you were okay. I said some tough things to you yesterday—things I regret."

"Like what?"

"Like not wanting to see you again until you'd gotten this stone business out of your head."

"I understand why you're afraid of that," he murmured, tracing the shape of her cheek with his thumb.

"I'm not anymore, Abel. Why or how you love me doesn't matter anymore. I'm ready."

Abel froze above her, his gaze sharply seeking hers. "Do you mean that?"

She nodded, shaky suddenly, now that the time had come to expose her true feelings. "When you played Indiana Jones at the Persephone Club, I should have realized how much you must care for me. But when I came in here just a few minutes ago and saw you risking your life—well, no other man would have done what you did unless he really cared."

"I love you," he said huskily. "With all my heart."

She smiled and smoothed a wet lock of dark hair off his forehead. "I know that."

When he kissed her, his mouth tasted warm and delicious. He threaded his hands into her hair and aligned his body so they were intimately entwined. Samantha's thoughts took a nosedive into sensual delights, and she savored the kiss long after it was over.

When she opened her eyes, Abel was smiling. He said, "You came halfway around the world for some reason besides saving my neck the way you did just now."

"Yes, " said Samantha. "I came to tell you that I don't care about the stone."

"You mean—?"

"I don't care where the magic comes from, as long as it stays where it belongs—in both our hearts. I love you, Abel."

Samantha laughed as he seized her, joy lighting his features.

"You mean it, Samantha?" He started kissing her face, her neck. "You don't think I'm crazy anymore?"

"That remains to be seen. Anyway, it's a rather appealing kind of crazy."

He smiled into her eyes. "What are you doing?"

By their own volition, Samantha's fingers seemed to have traveled to the buttons on his shirt. "We should get you out of these wet clothes."

"Samantha—"

The buttons parted easily. "I'm here to protect you from all kinds of dangers," she murmured. "You could catch a cold."

"Miss Wyatt," he said, playing at being stern. "I think you're trying to seduce me."

"I've missed you," she whispered, tugging his head down so she could kiss his mouth. "I want to be with you."

He accepted her kisses graciously, smiling. "You don't strike me as the type who'd want to make love in a public place."

"It's not very public," she said, peeling the soaked shirt off his shoulders and noting that he helped with the maneuver. He threw it aside, and she said, "The whole island of Kimi Lau shuts down to watch *Santa Barbara*. We have an hour."

"And what do you propose to do in that hour? I can't imagine—"

She used both hands to smooth down his trousers, a caress that effectively stopped Abel in midsentence. To answer his question, she used her mouth to communicate exactly what she wanted. Slowly she kissed his lips, then trailed more across his stubble-rough face. Slowly she unfastened his belt.

Abel's hands roved expertly over her body, brushing caresses and covering her soft flesh with kisses. Samantha lay on the lava rock and wondered if she'd ever been in a more comfortable spot. The sea breeze wafted down the steps, filling the cave with a fine, sweet mist.

Abel felt like shouting. Or weeping—he couldn't be sure which, but the effect was the same. Though his throat felt tight with emotion, he managed to say, "I love you, Samantha."

Her green eyes were shining as she looked up at him. "I love you, Abel. Let me show you how much."

Abel groaned as Samantha finished undressing him. When his clothes were in a sodden heap nearby, she began to work a kind of magic that made his head spin. Time and again, she coaxed him to a new height of passion, only to back off and start all over again. Her tongue played insistent games, then her fingertips soothed him until his heart stopped pounding. At first she would not allow him to touch her in return, but soon her face was flushed with desire, and he managed to tug her blouse off. Her lace bra, both prim and erotic, drove him to fondle her breasts.

"In all your travels," she asked on a gasp, "have you ever made love in a hot tub?"

Abel glanced at the shimmering green pool of water, just a few yards away. "There's a first time for everything."

"Let's," she whispered in his ear.

First he wanted her as naked as he was. But Abel's fingers fumbled so badly he couldn't manage to get her clothes off by himself. Samantha laughed and did the job herself, standing up to shed her slim slacks and delicate panties. Appreciatively Abel watched her remove the garments one by one. Eventually Samantha's slender body was bathed in the golden glow of the setting sun and wreathed in mist.

"Darling, you're so beautiful. You hardly look real."

"Touch me," she said, her voice trembling.

He put his hands on her flesh and found her skin hot beneath his palms. A feverish flush colored her face and throat.

He stood and pulled her by the hand. "Come with me."

The pool of luminous green water beckoned. It was still warm from the geyser and felt delightfully erotic. Abel slid into it first, and he almost wondered why his hot flesh didn't sizzle when it met the water. Samantha slipped into his arms, and they floated as if suspended in a scented bath.

Samantha wound her arms around his neck and moved her body against his. Her breasts brushed his chest, the nipples burning twin spots of flame where they touched him. Her smooth belly rubbed his, her thighs seemed to pull him closer. If the earth broke open and swallowed the two of them at that moment, Abel was sure neither of them would notice. He felt as if he could drown in the green depth of her eyes. All his senses were attuned to her, homing in on Samantha as if nothing else mattered. Her smile was intoxicating.

"Have you ever done this before?" she said with a wicked gleam in her eye.

"Once," he said, trying to memorize the look of desire in her eyes. "With the most erotic woman I've ever met. How about you?"

"I did once. It was with the sexiest man in the world. He made me think of doing things that never entered my head before."

Abel grinned. "Like what?"

"Like licking chocolate pudding—"

Laughing, he asked, "What else never entered your head?"

She slid out of his arms and rolled in the warm water like a lithe otter. "This. Are you ready?"

"And willing."

"Very willing, I notice."

As her mouth and fingertips played more caresses, Abel groaned and laughed at the same time. But he couldn't resist the temptation she offered. He chased her across the pool, the two of them gliding through the eerie green light in a game of tag more exciting than Abel had ever known. Watching Samantha's naked limbs slick with water, her hair coiling around her shoulders, her lips wet and parted, he knew he'd never dream about another woman again as long as he lived.

At last, he pinned her against the rocks. Eyes closed to savor the moment, he found her breasts with his lips and teased the nipples with his tongue. Samantha held his head, her own thrown back so she could breathe the cool air around them. Abel covered her body with caresses, as if trying to draw her picture on herself. He tickled her ribs and made her laugh again just to hear the sound of her rich voice in the hollow-sounding cave.

Still laughing, she turned over on her belly to escape the tickles. The sight of her back was just as stimulating as any other angle. Abel caught her before she could swim away. Samantha held still, waiting, her body floating in the water.

Kneading the sculpted curve of her bottom with his hands, Abel parted her thighs and found a small, willing target for his fingertip caresses. He pressed kisses down the back of her neck and felt her pulse beat wildly in her throat. Samantha writhed beneath him, her body arching as her excitement grew. Biting her ear gently, he brought her to the brink of climax, then found his way inside her.

Samantha made a soft sound when he thrust deeply into her warmth. Around them, the water eddied, licking, brushing, coaxing, to heighten their pleasure. Abel moved inside her again and again, but the splash was too distracting they started to laugh once more.

She turned in his arms, her face alight with pleasure. "I wish we could go on like this forever."

"We can. We will."

"Because of the stone?"

"I threw the stone away."

Samantha started in his arms, tilting her head to look up into his face. "Why?"

"Because it was important to you. And I—well, I didn't need it anymore."

She nestled pensively against his chest in the warm pool. "Do you believe in magic, Abel, really?"

"I believe in you and me. If that's magic, then I'm a sucker, I guess."

"Usually I'm one of those people who wants to know how the magician's tricks are done. I like solid facts."

"So do I. But I've learned that sometimes there aren't any answers. In my line of work, I have to go with my instincts when I'm not sure."

"And your instincts say—"

"That I love you. That I want to be with you. Forever."

Troubled, she whispered, "But tomorrow—"

"Tomorrow will come, but things won't be any different between us unless we let it happen that way. I won't give you up, Samantha. I can't."

As if to convince her of that truth, Abel moved to the threshold of sweet, agonizing pleasure. Slowly he sank inside her.

"I'm a part of you, Samantha," he murmured as his first deep thrust became a second and a third. "For as long as we live."

If the first time they made love was wild and wonderfully erratic, this time was gentler, slower—and infinitely more delicious. At precisely the moment he longed to hear her voice again, Samantha cried out—calling his name at the instant he propelled her into the wonderful plane between fantasy and reality. He loved listening to her abandon herself to the climax he gave her. When she called to him again, her voice was huskier still. And the third time, he joined her cries, plunging into a wonderful abyss with Samantha in his arms.

They melded, suspended as one body, two intermingling souls, a pair of spirits that broke the barrier of flesh to become one.

Samantha clung to Abel, half afraid to open her eyes for fear they had fallen through the water pool to a completely new world. She felt him kiss her lips again, then her cheeks and temples.

"My love," he murmured. "How do you feel? Half drowned?"

"No, just wonderfully at peace. We'll never have a chance like this again, will we?"

"I think I know who to talk to about renting the place for our honeymoon."

Samantha sat up slowly. "Abel . . ."

He lay comfortably in the water, his eyes dark as he admired her bare body. "Yes, love? You have something against honeymoons?"

"Abel—"

"Or something against what comes a few hours before the honeymoon?"

"Darling," Samantha said, striving to sound logical, "how long have we known each other?"

"Does it matter? We've been apart all our lives, but we know we belong together now. On your dance card of life, I'm the only name written down and you know it. I say we get married."

Samantha laughed. "You were ready to do that the night we met."

"I've always been a quick study. What do you say? Can you stand to be married to a guy like me?"

"We haven't even learned what we've got in common! Do you like Chinese food? Vacations at the beach or in the mountains? Do you vote Democrat or Republican?"

"Last time I voted," he said proudly, "I think Nixon was running. For vice president."

"Oh, my God!" Aghast, Samantha cried, "How can I marry a man who doesn't even vote?"

"The same way I can marry a woman who probably doesn't like parachuting."

"Parachuting!"

"My favorite sport. But I'm not going to force it on you. I firmly believe we'll get along fine if we draw the lines early. Life will be interesting, that's all."

Smiling, Samantha studied his face. "I'll bet you're never ambivalent about anything, are you? You make your decision and never waver."

"Same as you," he said. "Am I right?"

Wagging her head, Samantha said, "We could have a very exciting marriage, Abel."

"Then you'll do it? Be my wife?"

"Yes. I have a feeling it will be a challenge domesticating you, but—"

"But you love a challenge," Abel said, pulling her close once more.

They kissed and played in the water, but eventually the sun set completely, leaving them in semidarkness. By the rising moon, they dressed themselves. Shortly thereafter, a canoe arrived to take them to back to Kimi Lau.

Abel went out to speak to the man who owned the canoe. As Samantha bent to retrieve her shoes, she saw a small object glinting on the floor of the cave. She picked it up instinctively.

And found herself staring at Abel's magic stone.

"What in the world is this doing here?"

She figured it must have been blown back into the cave by the geyser. For a second, Samantha considered turning and hurling it back, sending the silly piece of rock back to the god who empowered it. But something stopped her.

With a secret smile, she tucked the stone into her pocket.

Samantha had taken a room at the island's only hotel—a small, ramshackle place with screen doors, no air conditioning and room service that only supplied hot rice and beer after nine p.m. For lack of more romantic amusements, she took Abel into her bed where they made love for half the night and spent the other half talking.

In the morning, Abel agreed to go back to civilization—or at least an island with a few more amenities. A telephone call to Washington bought Samantha a few days of vacation.

Speaker Glendenning took the call himself. "Where are you?"

"I'm not telling you," said Samantha. "This is one trip I won't let politics interrupt."

"We've got business to take care of! Constituents to serve! Samantha, I need you!"

"And I need this time off."

Gruffly, the Speaker asked, "Are you alone?"

She couldn't keep the smile from her voice. "Not exactly."

"What? Who's with you? Not young Fletcher!" The Speaker hooted triumphantly. "By golly, I knew that boy had gumption!"

"And a great deal more," Samantha said. "Goodbye, sir. I'll be back someday."

With a grin, Abel took her hand as she hung up the phone. "Care for a stroll before we hit the airport and your first lesson in happy flying?"

"A stroll sounds like a wonderful idea."

The sun was shining, and the air smelled like the ocean. Together, they strolled down the main thoroughfare of Kimi Lau's capital city, a muddy path lined with a few carts filled with island fare and a few trinkets made by the natives. A throng of Kimi Lauan people were enjoying market day.

Samantha exclaimed over a few carved statues and politely admired the pig one eager farmer thrust in her path. Abel firmly pushed through the crowd but suddenly stopped dead in the middle of the road.

"Good Lord!"

Samantha peeked over his shoulder to see a plump little man in Bermuda shorts blocking Abel's progress. "Who is this?" she asked, noting the startled expressions on both men. "Someone you know, darling?"

For a second, the little man looked appalled to find himself standing in front of Abel, but he seemed to catch himself and straightened his posture. A noble look soon appeared on his face. His chin lifted, his gaze grew imperious. Though he was dressed like a tourist just back from Disneyland, he acted like the prince of all he surveyed.

"This," said Abel, eyeing the ludicrous figure with distaste, "is King Kimimungo—the man who gave me the magic stone."

The King's face split into a wily grin as he caught sight of Samantha. "Aha!" he crowed. "Love charm worked for big American hero!"

Abel glowered. "Damn right it did—not that I needed it in the first place."

Samantha stepped forward and put out her hand for the King to shake. "How do you do, Your Highness? I'm delighted to meet you."

Grinning, the King shook Samantha's hand. "You like love charm, pretty lady?"

"It's been very exciting, I must say."

"You want more?" the King asked with a gap-toothed smile. "Maybe a charm to bring you good luck? Or a man with more virility?"

Laughing, Samantha said, "No, I think I've got my hands full already."

The King stood back to reveal the cartload of trinkets behind him. With a sweeping gesture, he invited Samantha closer. "I have charms for everything under the sun! See anything you like? It is yours for a present! I give away many charms. It's good business."

Samantha stared at the cartload of little painted stones exactly like the one that had turned her life upside down. Making a small noise in the back of his throat, Abel stepped closer, stunned by the sight of thousands of magic love charms.

"Here," said King Kimimungo, snatching up one of the stones and pressing it into Samantha's hand, "take this one, pretty lady. No charge! Very powerful magic. You will have twelve sons with this charm."

Samantha dropped it like a hot potato. "No thanks," she said weakly.

"Too late," said the King with a huge smile. "Magic works as soon as you touch the stone." He put one arm around Samantha and threw the other one around Abel's shoulders. "Very happy family, right?"

Abel began to laugh. "Right," he said. "Very happy."

*   *   *   *   *

Take 4 bestselling love stories FREE

Plus get a FREE surprise gift!

SILHOUETTE·INTIMATE·MOMENTS®

Premiering this month, a captivating new cover for Silhouette's most adventurous series!

Every month, Silhouette Intimate Moments sweeps you away with four dramatic love stories rich in passion. Silhouette Intimate Moments presents love at its most romantic, where life is exciting and dreams do come true.

Look for the new cover this month, wherever you buy Silhouette® books.

2IMNC-1A

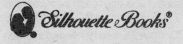 *Silhouette Books®*

Win 1 of 10 Romantic Vacations and Earn Valuable Travel Coupons Worth up to $1,000!

Inside every Harlequin or Silhouette book during September, October and November, you will find a PASSPORT TO ROMANCE that could take you around the world.

By sending us the official entry form available at your favorite retail store, you will automatically be entered in the PASSPORT TO ROMANCE sweepstakes, which could win you a star-studded London Show Tour, a Caribbean Cruise, a fabulous tour of France, a sun-drenched visit to Hawaii, a Mediterranean Cruise or a wander through Britain's historical castles. The more entry forms you send in, the better your chances of winning!

In addition to your chances of winning a fabulous vacation for two, valuable travel discounts on hotels, cruises, car rentals and restaurants can be yours by submitting an offer certificate (available at retail stores) properly completed with proofs-of-purchase from any specially marked PASSPORT TO ROMANCE Harlequin® or Silhouette® book. The more proofs-of-purchase you collect, the higher the value of travel coupons received!

For details on your PASSPORT TO ROMANCE, look for information at your favorite retail store or send a self-addressed stamped envelope to:

PASSPORT TO ROMANCE
P.O. Box 621
Fort Erie, Ontario L2A 5X3

 ONE PROOF-OF-PURCHASE   3-CSD-1

To collect your free coupon booklet you must include the necessary number of proofs-of-purchase with a properly completed offer certificate available in retail stores or from the above address.